DEDICATION

*To my mom, all the COVID-19 victims,
including Dr. Susan Moore, and all the kind
healthcare workers who are working hard
and doing the right thing.*

*This book is also dedicated to the
six Asian women who were the victims of a
deadly hate crime in Atlanta, Georgia on
March 16th, 2021. You are gone,
but never forgotten.*

ACKNOWLEDGMENTS

I want to acknowledge my mom, who died in 2014 from stomach and colon cancer. She was a strong and courageous woman who worked so hard to raise her seven children. She put up a good fight until her last breath. My mom believed in hard work and kindness, and she was my lifetime teacher.

I also want to thank my childhood friend, Jongwha, and her family in South Korea. They kept me sane throughout the COVID-19 pandemic.

Lastly, I want to thank my copy editor, Taryn Wieland, as well as all the Online Book Club Members, who have given me an honest and helpful criticism of my book before its release.

AUTHOR'S NOTE

COVID-19 has affected everyone worldwide, reshaping how we live our lives in countless ways. It has also given us an opportunity to take a closer look at what we have taken for granted, as well as discuss problems that everyone has spent years ignoring in the hope of maintaining the status quo. If we've learned anything through this experience, it's that there are no guarantees in life, and we are all connected to each other more than we've ever realized.

There have been many courageous and heartwarming stories of communities pulling together to help each other out. Unfortunately, there have also been darker, more horrific stories. Many are learning that where we live and the industries we work within are not as free from intolerance, racism, and bullying as we would expect them to be. I hope this book offers some comfort and inspiration to readers who seek solutions for racial injustices and discrimination. I also hope this book allows you to re-examine and reflect on how you treat others and carry yourself daily.

Unfortunately, the medical profession is not immune to racism, coupled with corruption and white privilege. Non-Caucasian nurses across the country have been affected by the pain of discrimination, harassment, bullying, and targeting. Over the years, foreign nurses have played a pivotal role in the United States healthcare system. Significantly, during the 1980s, foreign nurses were imported to take care of AIDS and HIV patients throughout the U.S. Back then, AIDS was a deadly, misunderstood disease that was seen as incurable. Many American nurses refused to care for AIDS and HIV-positive patients, which made the nursing shortage worse. As a result, the U.S. government decided to import foreign nurses, mostly from the Philippines, South Korea, Japan, India, Mexico, Thailand, the United Kingdom, Germany, Trinidad, Tobago, Jamaica, and Canada. Among them, it was mainly the nurses of color who had to take care of AIDS and HIV patients.

Despite all the hard work contributed by nurses of color, the stigma of racism overshadowed their crucial contribution to the U.S. government and its people. These nurses were forced to silence their work-related racial discrimination for fear of losing their jobs or being blacklisted in the nursing profession.

As a registered nurse in the U.S., I have experienced and witnessed others being discriminated against by co-workers, employers, and patients throughout my career, regardless of where I worked. It has been painful and absolutely heartbreaking.

As the whole world spoke of pulling together and talked about weathering the same storm, things only got worse for front-line nurses. Stress levels and discrimination only intensified during the COVID-19 pandemic in the healthcare profession. I was so horrified by everything I witnessed that I felt compelled to shine a light on it in this fictional form to help raise awareness about the direness of the situation.

CHAPTER 1

Kirkland, Washington
March 10, 2020

Ginger Kim awoke as she felt her body being lifted onto a gurney. She struggled to open her eyes, but couldn't. Ginger could hear anxious voices around her. It was the paramedics she had called when she couldn't breathe, just before she had collapsed.

"I've seen her before, in the Emergency Department. She's a nurse," the man who had given her oxygen said to his partner.

"We're all going to get this thing before it's through," the other man replied, a tinge of anger in his voice.

"She said something about not taking her to Pine Health. She asked to go to UW Medical instead. But we can't take any chances bypassing Pine Health, she's too sick. Thanks to the oxygen we gave her, she just regained consciousness, but she's not out of the woods yet. We need to take her to Pine Health now," the first man said.

Ginger could feel the jolt as they lifted her gurney into the back of a waiting ambulance.

"I wonder why she would make such a request?"

"I don't know. She wasn't making sense—something about her previous bosses and co-workers being evil to her four years ago."

"Hmm. Well, she can request to be transferred out after she gets to the ED."

"Or her family can make that request later. Let's hurry!"

Ginger wanted to tell them that she needed to be transferred out immediately. She wasn't hallucinating—she just didn't have enough energy to convince them. Even with the non-rebreather mask, Ginger was barely getting enough oxygen to stay conscious. She wanted to tell them that she needed to go somewhere else, somewhere safe, where no one would tarnish her name and frame her. Somewhere they wouldn't let her die…

…just because she was Korean.

Gwangju, South Korea
October 27, 1979

Something was wrong. Thirteen-year-old Ginger stood shoulder-to-shoulder with her best friend, Eungi, on the playground of Gwangju Middle School. All 1,300 students stood at attention in their black uniforms. Both boys and girls wore black long-sleeved tops, though the boys wore pants and the girls wore skirts.

Ginger picked at her clothes nervously, even though she was trying not to move.

Across from her and all the other students were their teachers. They stood, grim-faced, unmoving, unspeaking. Principal Shim was going to address the students, which was highly unusual since he usually saved such speeches for Mondays rather than Saturdays, which were only half days. Something bad had happened. Ginger could feel it in the air.

"Do you know what's going on?" Eungi whispered.

Ginger stared straight ahead and elbowed her friend slightly. Talking wasn't permitted while they were assembled, and given the strangeness of the situation, she was sure they'd get in even more trouble than usual for such an infraction. She just shook her head a little.

She didn't know what was going on, but she was sure it couldn't be good.

Finally, Principal Shim, an older man with glasses, took his place on a metal stage that was two feet off the ground. Everyone could see him clearly as he stood there for a moment, surveying them. Ginger thought she saw his hands shaking. Then he wrapped his fingers around the edge of a light-brown wooden podium, gripping it tightly.

Despite his frail appearance, he garnered great respect. Principal Shim was a hero, having fought the Japanese occupation that had ended in 1945. He faced his young students now with a somberness to him that was more intense than Ginger ever remembered seeing. He cleared his throat.

"I'm sure some of you are already aware of President Park's assassination. Tragically, he was killed last night."

Ginger, Eungi, and half the others in the assembly gasped. She tried to suppress it, but the news shocked her. Who would want to kill the president?

"This is our national tragedy," Principal Shim continued. "But we must not be shaken by the tragic situation. You must continuously study hard and focus on your duties as students. You are our future, the future of our Republic of Korea."

Ginger felt that responsibility settle down on her shoulders. There was nothing she could do for the president, but she could do something for her country. Her country needed her to be a good student. She had always taken her schoolwork seriously, but now she felt like she needed to do more, be better.

She glanced at Eungi, whose eyes were full of fear. Eungi was also a good student, and Ginger could tell she was feeling the same burden to do better.

Everyone around her was silent. No one seemed to even breathe, let alone move.

Things have changed, Ginger thought. Somehow, this moment in time had shifted everything. She just prayed that things would get better and not worse.

As Principal Shim dismissed them and sent them to their classes, Ginger listened to the hushed conversations around her.

"My father said he was killed by his best friend, Kim Jaegyu," one boy said grimly.

"Why would he do that?" the boy walking beside him asked.

Ginger reached out impulsively and grabbed Eungi's hand. Eungi squeezed hers back. Ginger could never imagine hurting Eungi, not for anything. She could feel her heart beating painfully fast as they walked into the building.

They began to move to their different classes, slowly and reluctantly. It was as though they all somehow wanted to stay together in the face of what had just happened and whatever was coming next. Ginger wanted to go home. She wanted to run into her parents' arms. Somehow, hugging them would make her feel better—it always did.

She saw her teacher walk into their classroom, her face stoic just as all the other teachers' faces had been while the principal was speaking.

"It will be alright," a gentle voice said.

Ginger turned to see who had spoken. The school nurse was standing in front of her room, her face filled with a calm and serene expression. She had her hand on the shoulder of one of the youngest girls who was crying. The nurse raised her head and met Ginger's eyes. She smiled, as if to say that it really was going to be all right.

Ginger took a deep, shuddering breath and she smiled back.

CHAPTER 2

Kirkland, Washington
March 10, 2020

"We are testing you for COVID-19, among other things," she heard a voice telling her.

After a few moments' struggle, Ginger was able to open her eyes.

Dr. Tan was standing over her. Ginger felt a little bit of relief. At least it wasn't Dr. Koppel, who would disappear with one of the nurses or technicians to have sex while they were both on duty, or Dr. Hart, whose malpractice had forced Ginger to go to extraordinary lengths to single-handedly save a patient's life.

"Can you hear me?" Dr. Tan asked.

"Yes," Ginger answered, her voice gravelly and nearly unrecognizable even to her.

"I need to ask you some questions," Dr. Tan said, her eyes expressing her concern.

Ginger nodded.

"When did you begin to feel ill?"

"A…few…days…ago…But…I… had to…work…anyway. My… manager…did not… allow… me…to… take… a… sick day. He…said…as long…as…I…don't…have a…fever, I…

must…come…to…work." Ginger struggled to catch her breath. Talking was nearly impossible.

"I…felt…fatigued…after…a… shower. I… couldn't…breathe. I…called…for an… ambulance."

"It's a good thing you did. I won't ask you any more questions since you are short of breath." Dr. Tan said, shaking her head. "Your oxygen was only 80%. Your heart rate was 138. You're lucky to be alive."

Gwangju, South Korea
May 2, 1980

I *am lucky to be alive*, Ginger pondered, as she sat huddled in the corner of the family room of her parents' home. Two of her neighborhood friends, Misoon and Yeoni, hadn't been so lucky. The thirteen and eleven-year-old sisters had been killed in their own home by bullets that had struck them when they were standing at a window. Their parents had found them dead. Ginger had heard that after being shot by one of General Jun's thugs, Yeoni's head had been partially missing. All the neighbors had been horrified at the sight of their death and terrified of the power of the rifle. A month later, her friends' parents were still mourning and wailing. Neighbors wept whenever they heard their pain-stricken cries.

"Darling, stay away from the windows," Ginger's mother told her worriedly.

Thirteen-year-old Ginger began to worry that she might never be able to look out a window again. She kept having recurring nightmares that her brother, Daehan, would finally return from the university, only to be killed on their doorstep before she could see him. Before she could tell him how much she'd missed him all these months they'd been apart.

Daehan attended the aviation engineering school in Inchon. It was the only specialized university in the country, which President Park had established for the specific purpose of gaining military independence from the U.S. Ginger and her entire family had all been so proud and excited when Daehan passed the difficult entrance exam and was accepted into the university.

Now, because General Jun had closed all the universities, Daehan was coming home. Students from all 37 universities had been participating in demonstrations against Jun since he'd overthrown Chea Gyuha, who had been acting president for less than two months following President Park's assassination.

Ever since the demonstrations started, Ginger's parents had been worried about their son, and their fear had transmitted to her. She had overheard them talking on more than one occasion about the atrocities Jun's soldiers were committing against the student demonstrators. They hadn't known from day to day whether Daehan was safe. But now that his university was officially closed, he'd be coming home. They'd all get to see with their own eyes that he was all right.

At least, Ginger desperately hoped he was. As fear gnawed at her, she decided to call Eungi. For weeks, her only contact with her best friend had been over the phone. As much as Ginger missed seeing her, she was thankful that they were still able to talk.

She went to the phone and picked up the black receiver. She felt better just knowing that she would soon be talking to Eungi.

Having someone her own age to discuss things with made it all seem better somehow.

But as she lifted the receiver to her ear, she froze. There was no dial tone. She realized with horror that what her parents had been worrying about for days had finally happened. General Jun had disabled the phones.

After staying frozen for a while, Ginger carefully put the receiver back before she plopped down on the floor. She then wrapped her arms around herself, her chest tightening as she realized that she was completely cut off from the rest of the world. Not being able to communicate with her friends made her feel even more isolated.

Ginger wanted to go outside on the street and see what was really going on with her own eyes, even though it wasn't safe to do so. She hadn't been outside in almost six weeks, and now she couldn't even talk to her best friend on the phone. It felt like the walls were closing in on her, and she wanted to scream.

You can't go outside, she reminded herself, trying to breathe through her own panic. *It's not safe. If you go outside, you could die.*

These words had been repeated to Ginger by both her parents until she heard them in her dreams. She longed to breathe fresh air, to feel the sun on her face. She wanted to see her best friend and hug her. But she couldn't. Now, she couldn't even talk to her.

Tears began to well in Ginger's eyes and slowly roll down her cheeks. She didn't know how much longer this would go on. It felt like the entire world had fallen apart and was never going to get put back together.

She sat down, tucking her knees up under her chin. She wrapped her arms around her legs and rocked slowly, trying to calm herself. She closed her eyes tightly and tried to imagine that she was somewhere else, that she was safe and happy and free. She imagined her friends and family were there with her.

Suddenly, a commotion at the front door snapped her out of her daydream. She opened her eyes and took a deep breath.

"He's here!" she heard her mother shout in relief.

Ginger jumped to her feet, wiped the tears from her eyes, and ran to greet her brother. When she made it to the door, she hung back, heeding her mother's warnings not to get too close to the window.

Finally, Daehan came inside with two others, a boy and a girl who were both his age. All three of them were carrying large bags that they carefully placed on the floor. Daehan also had a backpack and a large box, which he carefully deposited on the floor.

Ginger's mother quickly closed the door and welcomed them all further into the house. Once safely away from windows and doors, she threw her arms around her son and hugged him like she had just discovered he was back from the dead.

When she let go, Ginger ran forward and wrapped her arms around her brother's waist.

"Brother! I'm so glad you are home!"

"I missed you too, sis," Daehan said warmly.

She nodded, struggling to hold back a fresh wave of tears. Daehan was here, and he was safe. That made everything better. She felt hope blossom inside her. Finally, she stepped back and allowed her brother to greet their father.

"Mom, Dad, I'd like you to meet my friends from school. This is Yusung and Mira," he said, introducing the boy and girl next to him. "These are my parents and my sister, Ginger."

Ginger nodded politely. She'd heard Daehan talk about Yusung and Mira before.

"You are most welcome in our house," Ginger's father said.

Yusung and Mira thanked him in unison. Ginger noticed, though, that her brother and his friends all wore strained, anxious looks. They acted like they were constantly waiting for something to happen. She'd seen a similar look on boys in her class when they pulled a prank and were just waiting to be caught. Only there was no excitement or hilarity in her brother and his two friends' eyes. There was more of a grim determination, mixed with anger and sadness.

"Tell us everything," her father said.

"Over dinner," her mother added, leading the way toward the dining area.

Ginger's mother had been cooking since early morning, anticipating the arrival of her son. Whether her parents had been expecting Daehan to bring friends, Ginger didn't know. She did know that her mother had made enough food to feed a small army, so there would be plenty for all.

CHAPTER 3

Kirkland, Washington
March 10, 2020

"We don't have enough!" Dr. Tan blurted out.

Ginger was still struggling to keep her wits about her as she stared up at the doctor.

"What?" she asked weakly.

"Beds. We're filled up here. I'm gonna have to transfer you out to downtown Seattle."

For a while, Ginger had forgotten which ED she was in. All her energy was focused on her breathing. No matter how much she tried to breathe, she felt like she could never get enough oxygen in her lungs.

She was very glad to hear she was being transferred to a different hospital without having to explain herself any further. It was a huge relief that the nurses here wouldn't be responsible for her care.

"You have all the symptoms of COVID-19," Dr. Tan explained. "So until we know otherwise, we need to treat you as though that's what you have. As you know, it will take seven to ten days to get your test results back."

Ginger nodded again. She knew exactly what this was all about. She also knew that quarantine required fourteen days. She had seen firsthand the frustration of her patients and their families when they were put in fourteen days of isolation at Alderwood Medical Center. However, in that moment, as she kept fighting to breathe, Ginger felt that she wouldn't last even another five minutes.

Gwangju, South Korea
May 17, 1980

Ginger didn't know what was happening around her, but she did know that things had gotten much worse in the two weeks since Daehan had been home. He and his friends from college were part of a militia that was working to keep their neighborhood and their city safe.

But "safe" seemed to be a relative term these days. Ginger heard whispers about the things happening outside her home. Daehan and the others would take turns going up on the roof of her parents' house to stand watch. They'd take rifles and walkie-talkies with them. The walkie-talkies were wrapped in foil so that the military couldn't pick up the signals. At least, that's what Daehan had told their parents.

At dinner that evening, they all discussed the fact that General Jun's troops were getting more violent by the day. It seemed to Ginger that there were some things Daehan would start to mention, but would stop, look at her, and say something else instead. She didn't know what it meant, but she knew he was trying to protect her from hearing things he didn't think she should.

But no one can protect anyone.

At least, that was the fear that had been slowly growing in her by the day. No matter what Daehan and his friends did, things weren't getting any better. They were simply outnumbered. There wasn't enough her parents could do to protect Daehan, and that thought terrified Ginger.

It was long past Ginger's bedtime, but she lingered in the living room. Daehan emerged from his room, rifle in hand, and she approached him. Through the door behind him, she could see into his room where half a dozen boys and young men were sleeping on the floor.

Mira and three other girls had been sleeping on the floor in Ginger's room for the last few days. It made Ginger even more nervous, especially since a couple of them had guns. But Ginger's parents had explained to her that housing and feeding members of the militia was their duty.

It seemed like everyone was using the word "duty" lately. She knew her parents were taking their role seriously. Her mother practically never left the kitchen as she cooked endless food for Daehan and the other militia members, including many who weren't staying at their house but would drop by for food and supplies.

"What are you doing up, sis?" Daehan asked Ginger softly, trying not to disturb those who were sleeping. He carefully closed the door and stepped away from it.

"Brother, I wanted to see you," she said, anxiety twisting in her stomach.

He smiled at her, and for a moment, she saw the version of her brother that she best remembered. With a smile in his eyes, Daehan looked fearless, carefree, yet determined.

"Okay, you've seen me. Now off to bed."

He was teasing her. It should have made her feel better, but somehow, it just made her fears worse.

"Not…not yet," she stammered, wishing she could easily tell him everything that was in her heart.

"What is it, sis?" he asked, his smile fading.

Ginger stood there, looking up at him as so many thoughts crowded her mind. She wanted to tell him how much she loved him. She wanted to beg him not to go on watch. She wished the nightmare that they were living would just go away. When she was little and would skin her knee or sprain her ankle, he'd always been there with a hug to make her feel better. But no hug could fix what was wrong now.

"Well…sis, when you're ready to talk, let me know," he said, moving toward the front of the house.

"I don't want you to get hurt," she blurted out.

Daehan stopped and turned to look at her, his face now serious.

Daehan asked Ginger, "What's making you so sensitive today? Is it because I'm about to go on watch? Don't worry, I've done this for the past two weeks without a problem."

Ginger shrugged, not wanting to admit that she'd had nagging feelings of dread for the entirety of those two weeks.

He smiled at her. "I'm not going to get hurt, sis."

"You don't know that…" Ginger countered. She picked at her clothes, growing more nervous as she talked about her fear.

His smile slowly faded. "You're right. I don't. But even if I do get hurt, it's okay."

"How can you say that?"

"Because I'll get hurt doing the right thing. Sometimes, sacrifices have to be made to heal a people, a nation. Someone has to stand up and do the right thing, regardless of the cost. Do you understand?"

"I...I don't know...Isn't there a better way to fix what's broken?"

"Not when you're dealing with tyrants like General Jun."

"Can't you tell me what it's all about?" Ginger pleaded. She had a vague notion, but her parents, the militia, and even Daehan talked around her about such things—never *to* her.

"Freedom," he said simply.

She looked around the house that she had been trapped in for months. "This is freedom?" she asked.

"No, it's not, and that's the point," her brother said sternly. "We want democracy and an end to martial law. We want freedom for the press so that ideas aren't suppressed. We should have basic human rights guaranteed to us. Jun and his type don't agree. They want to control everyone. They fear democracy." He shifted the rifle in his arm and sighed deeply. He gave her a weary smile, but the light of conviction shone in his eyes. "Okay, it's my turn up on the roof. We'll talk more tomorrow. Okay, little sis?"

"But tell me why, brother," she begged.

"I've already explained it to you," he said with a frown.

Ginger shook her head. "Why does it have to be *you*?"

"Because someone needs to stand up against injustice," he said slowly. "If I don't, who will?"

CHAPTER 4

Kirkland, Washington
March 10, 2020

Ginger needed to call someone before it was too late. Even as she asked for the phone, she felt darkness clawing at the corners of her mind.

Dr. Tan explained that they would be intubating Ginger as soon as she finished her call. That meant they'd be placing a breathing tube down her throat and hooking her up to a ventilator. The machine would take over her breathing function. It was a common procedure, but fear twisted her stomach as she struggled to think.

Who was she going to call? The answer was there…she knew it had to be. So many people she knew were dead. Maybe there was no one left to call.

She shook her head, struggling to clear it enough to think. She needed help. She needed to tell someone what was happening to her and where she was going.

"God, please help me," she prayed.

Gwangju, South Korea
May 18, 1980

Ginger wanted desperately to pray, but she felt as if all words had left her. The whole world was upside down and on fire. General Jun had pulled off a coup, ousting the acting president and instating martial law. The entire thing had taken less than ten minutes, or so she'd been told. She had no idea how long the aftermath was going to last.

Her brother, his friends, and half of their neighbors had taken to the streets downtown to protest. They wanted a free, democratic country—not another dictator.

"He's calling everyone who opposes him a communist," Ginger heard her father say worriedly from the other room. "That's not right."

"Who's a communist?" her mother asked, sounding almost bewildered at the thought. "Since when is democracy communism?"

"It's just an excuse to kill whoever gets in his way," her father answered.

Ginger heard her mother suck in her breath. Her mother was worried sick about Daehan. They all were.

A soft knock on the front door startled everyone into momentary silence. Ginger's father got up and answered. A moment later, one of their neighbors joined Ginger's parents in the kitchen.

Ginger stayed in the family room. She knew her parents didn't want her to hear how bad things were, but she needed to know if something happened to her brother.

"What have you heard?" Ginger's father asked, his voice low and tense.

"It's bad."

"How bad?" her mother asked.

"The protests have turned into war. Jun's soldiers are murdering everyone, old women, young children. They don't care. The American G.I. who are with them don't care either. The city is locked down. They are saying that we are all spies and deserve to be killed."

"How can they say that?" Ginger's mother burst out.

"It's madness. An eight-year-old girl who was running from the fighting was shot in the head when she stopped to retrieve her shoe. No one is safe."

"Aigoo, I feel so hopeless. I wish I could join Daehan, but my sixty-year-old legs will not carry me fast enough if I must run away from Jun's soldiers," Ginger's father said as if he was talking to himself, with a voice full of anxiety.

"There is no running. No hiding either. They shot a young woman in the stomach after they found her hiding in a shop downtown. She was eight months pregnant."

Ginger felt as though her heart would stop. Her stomach turned as she heard about Jun and his men so cruelly murdering innocent people.

"We must do something," Ginger's mother said, appealing to her husband.

"We can contribute food and water, and pray for Daehan and his friends' safe return. At the moment, I think that is all we can do," her father said in a less anxious voice.

"But how will we get the food and water to them?" her mother questioned.

"Where are the protestors most concentrated?" her father asked.

"They are everywhere downtown, but they have managed to take hold of the Jeonnam Provincial Government building. There is a great concentration of them there."

"I know that building well," her father said. "There is a side door I can reach without being easily seen by Jun's soldiers. I can use it to deliver food and water."

Ginger's father had been a building inspector for thirty-five years. She was sure her father could find a way in and out without being seen. That didn't scare her nearly as much as the thought of him being shot on the streets on his way to and from the building. She could feel her chest tighten as she imagined her father being killed just like the girl and the pregnant woman.

"How much food can you make?" the neighbor asked Ginger's mother.

"More than he can carry."

"I will find others to help," the neighbor promised.

"Good," Ginger's father said. "At least this way, we can do something to help."

Ginger wished there was something she could do to help. She knew her parents would never let her leave the house, even to help deliver food and water. They had already lectured her three times that day about staying hidden and not turning on the lights.

So, Ginger just sat in the corner of the family room, waiting and worrying. She had her rosary wrapped around her wrist, just as her parents wore theirs. Her mother had often told her that she could only ask God for one thing at a time, and that if she asked for too much at once, God might not grant her wish. She hoped that wasn't true, or at least God would make an exception.

Ginger got down on her knees, closed her eyes, and thought of Daehan downtown and her parents, who would be helping however they could. She thought of her own fears of being killed. Lastly, she thought of her best friend Eungi, who she wished she could talk to soon. Ginger wasn't sure if Eungi was safe or not. For all she knew, her friend might already be dead.

Tears squeezed through her eyelids as Ginger prayed for all of them and herself. She knew it was a lot, but she was desperate. God must understand that. Still, she felt the need to make sure. If He did this for her, then Ginger would do something for Him. Perhaps she could help people. Even heal them.

"God, if you help me, I'll commit to helping others when I grow up. I promise. In the name of the Father, the Son, and the Holy Spirit, amen."

CHAPTER 5

Kirkland, Washington
March 10, 2020

inger's mind cleared just enough as she prayed. She grasped the phone and managed to call her brother. Fortunately, Daehan answered quickly.

"I'm…sick. They're…intubating…me…and…sending…me… to…another… hospital," she explained, slurring her words. She told him where she was and had a vague idea that he repeated it. It was too hard to tell. All she could hear was the panic in his voice.

The phone slipped from her hand and she heard it hit the floor. She couldn't find the breath to ask someone to pick it up for her.

Ginger watched as a nurse inserted a second IV into a vein of her left arm. Moments later, white propofol started flowing into her body. They needed her sedated and unconscious so they could intubate her. She felt her eyes sliding closed. Some things were better to be unconscious for, and this was one of those times.

She felt a sensation of warmth and lightness. She slowly opened her eyes and looked down at herself. Doctors and nurses were scurrying around. She was on a ventilator. She wasn't sure when they'd gotten her completely hooked up. It was strange to watch the machine keep her body alive, and she struggled to feel connected to what was happening.

The warmth increased, and everything turned a brilliant white. She was somewhere else, standing in a field of wildflowers. Flowers swayed side to side from a gentle, warm breeze. Ginger turned and saw her parents smiling at her, waving, gesturing for her to join them. Ginger felt safe there. She couldn't remember the last time she'd felt so peaceful.

She realized that she was dying, but somehow, that was okay. Life had been filled with so much fear, so much pain. In that moment, she didn't know why she had feared death so much.

Gwangju, South Korea
May 27, 1980 - January 1, 1981

Hundreds were dead. Thousands were missing. The numbers were too horrible to comprehend as the Gwangju Democratization Movement was crushed by Jun's soldiers and the U.S. troops acting to support him.

Ginger had no idea if Eungi or any of her other friends from school were among the dead or missing. Worse, she had yet to hear news about her brother.

The front door opened, and she jumped up from her seat in the family room, her heart in her throat. Her father came in quickly, his face grim.

"What is the news?" her mother asked, hurrying to his side.

"Daehan, Yusung, and Mira have been arrested."

"Thank God they are alive," her mother said, bursting into tears.

Her father nodded. "For now. Word is that 60,000 have been arrested. They are to be locked up in isolated Samchunggyoyukdae."

"Surely they can't hold so many there," her mother said.

"That's what I'm afraid of," her father replied.

Ginger's heart sank. Her father was implying that instead of just trying to keep them imprisoned, Jun would have her brother and all those others killed.

"We have to help them," her mother whimpered.

"There is nothing we can do now but watch and wait," her father said.

Watch and wait. It seemed to become the mantra whereby Ginger lived her life. Or, rather, *didn't* live her life.

It had taken her weeks after Daehan and his friends' arrest to hear that her best friend also was alive. That realization had been joyous but short-lived as she realized that she still had no way to communicate with Eungi.

Finally, six months after Daehan's arrest, word came that Jun was going to close the Samchunggyoyukdae to save himself from being punished by the world human rights group.

On January 1st, Daehan walked through his parents' front door and they all rushed to greet him. Ginger almost didn't recognize her own brother. He looked completely different. His eye sockets were dark and sunken, and the hair on his head was completely shaved off. He wore summer clothing even though it was freezing cold. Ginger realized that he was still wearing what he wore on the day of his arrest. His clothes were ragged and covered with dried blood.

Ginger flinched. For a second, she wondered if the man standing in front of her was really her brother. His appearance reminded her of the devastating pictures she had seen in her world history textbook. She thought of those images of victims who had endured the concentration camps during World War II. Still, she knew it had to be him—her dear brother Daehan.

Ginger ran over, threw her arms around Daehan's stick-like waist, and hugged him. "Brother! Brother! You are back!" She didn't care how dirty and awful he looked. She was just so happy he had come back home alive.

Ginger's parents quietly embraced their son and hugged him for a long time. That's when Ginger noticed Daehan's missing three fingers on his right hand.

When she wept over his hand, he gave her a faint smile and told her to cheer up because it had been worse for so many others.

Then, Ginger's mother cheerfully made an announcement as she wiped away her tears, "We need to celebrate today as your second birthday, son! I'm going to cook everyone's favorite meal for dinner!"

Ginger's father brought Daehan some hot water to sip. "Your body will go into shock if you eat a full meal in your condition. Drink this water while I get ready for your bath. Go on, take a sip, son." Then, after gently stroking his son's bony back, he quietly walked towards the bathroom.

While Daehan sipped on the hot water and waited for the bathwater to be ready, Ginger saw her father weeping and wiping the tears off his face through the cracked space between the bathroom door and its casing. Though her father's crying was buried under the noise of running water, Ginger went into her room and cried along with him.

After Daehan finished his bath and dressed in a warm sweater and sweatpants, Yusung showed up, limping from the permanent nerve damage done to his right leg. He looked just as bad as Daehan, with the same shaved head and skin-and-bone appearance. Everyone embraced Yusung and welcomed him. Ginger's father served him hot water to drink.

"You rest here, son," Ginger's father softly said to Yusung. Then he prepared another hot bath.

The night was falling when Mira arrived, deaf in her right ear—the result of a soldier's beating. Her hair was filthy and matted, so much so that it seemed like it would be impossible to untangle. When Ginger and her mother helped Mira prepare for her bath, Ginger offered Mira an entire bottle of conditioner to help with her hair, and Mira finally uttered a few words to Ginger.

"Don't worry, Ginger. I can just cut it all off if I can't untangle it. It's just hair. It will grow back."

Ginger quietly nodded her head, her eyes still locked on Mira's hair, feeling bad for the choice she would have to make. The thought of Mira shaving all her hair off seemed unimaginable. Ginger had never seen a girl with a shaved head. It was uncustomary, with the exception of monks.

They had a feast with Bulgalbe, steamed rice, Kimchee, Miyeok-guk, with Miyeok-guk as the main dish. A seaweed-based soup, it was traditionally served on birthdays to wish health and longevity, but it seemed appropriate here as part of the celebratory feast.

It was a perfect homecoming as everyone sat around and enjoyed the delicious meal together. Ginger thought Mira's shaved head didn't look so bad after all. In fact, it looked much better than the matted hair she'd arrived with. Despite their injuries, they were all so happy to be back together, finally released from such a cruel, horrible place.

Even as they celebrated, something inside Ginger told her this joy wouldn't be long-lived.

"They will be spying on all of us now. I'm so sorry I brought this upon our family," Daehan told his parents after dinner.

His father lowered his voice and waved his hand. "They have been for months. Our phone calls are recorded. The police read all the mail that goes in and out."

"Mom, Dad, I'm so sorry I've brought this upon you," Daehan said, his sunken eyes sorrowful.

"No, do not be sorry, son. You stood up for what you believed in. Always be proud of that," his father said fiercely. "There will be consequences, yes, but we will deal with them."

As the days turned into weeks, those consequences became more obvious. Daehan had to give his daily schedule to the police. Ginger returned to school, but she was aware that she was followed wherever she went—even there. She had been writing in a diary that her mother had told her to hide, telling her that they could all be in real trouble if it was found. That scared Ginger because she'd thought they already *were* in real trouble.

The last straw for Daehan was when he wasn't allowed to get a job or go back to school because he had fought against Jun's coup. He felt suffocated by their near house-arrest situation, becoming increasingly hopeless. Daehan and his father stayed up late at night, discussing what he was going to do.

Then, early one morning, Daehan went into Ginger's room and woke her.

"Brother? What is it?" she asked, fear overtaking her.

"I've come to say goodbye, sis," he said solemnly.

"Where are you going, brother?" she asked as she struggled to comprehend what was happening.

"America. A place called Seattle. One of father's friends is the captain of a cargo ship, and he's offered to hire me as a deckhand and take me there. I'll finish my schooling in America and hopefully get an aviation job."

Both sorrow and excitement raced through Ginger.

"Can I come?" she asked.

"Not now. Hopefully soon," Daehan told her. "Until then, I'll communicate however I can. I love you, sis."

"I love you too, brother."

Daehan hugged his sister tightly. Ginger struggled to not let him see her cry, wanting to be as brave as him.

When Daehan left her room, she felt as though she was being torn apart. A minute later, she heard the front door open and close very softly. It was only then that Ginger realized her shoulder was wet with her brother's tears.

CHAPTER 6

Seattle, Washington
March 15, 2020

In ICU Room 301, Ginger Kim lay still in bed, intubated and unconscious as she had been for the past five days after being transferred from PHH ED.

Hyun, an ICU nurse, was working with the ECMO machine, which pumped blood out of Ginger's body, removed the carbon dioxide, oxygenated it, and then returned it to her body. The device was doing the work of Ginger's heart and lungs in cleaning and circulating the blood while the ventilator was oxygenating her lungs through the trachea.

Hyun checked that there were no kinks in the line or bubbles in the bright red blood. "It's going to be okay," she whispered to Ginger.

It was a harmless lie—words said to soothe her patient and herself. It was, of course, possible that Ginger would recover, but it wasn't looking good.

A team of medical personnel was crowded into the tiny space. Hyun ignored them and focused on her tasks, but Clara, the nurse working with her, was clearly nervous and hyper-aware of their presence.

Ginger's body looked like something out of a science-fiction novel, a horrible laboratory experiment meant to bring the dead back to life. Only, in her case, they were trying to keep the living from joining the dead.

She was wired up from head to toe. Three big IV lines branched out of the right side of the internal jugular vein in her neck, which connected to the multiple medications on the pole. The lines all originated from a single central port to inject all the critical medications effectively. In addition to the medications, there was a massive bag filled with a yellow-colored liquid, TPN, which was packed with nutrients, and pale white lipid in a separate, smaller sandwich-size bag.

Several wires connected Ginger to the cardiac monitor over her bed. The monitor indicated that her heart rate was 130 and her temperature was 102 Fahrenheit. Nothing seemed to be bringing either of those numbers down.

Greenish bile was being gently suctioned out of her stomach through her OG tube, running into the clear plastic canister fixed to the wall beside her. Near it, the two buttons, a blue one used to call for a code blue and a yellow button to call in the rapid response team, which was a standard room set-up for all hospital patients. However, the code buttons were now indispensable for Ginger since her life was hanging by a thread.

Hyun had her hands full with her job, but she kept glancing at Clara, the other nurse responsible for Ginger's care, except for the ECMO. Clara's face, as usual, was aged and withered from her long drinking habit. Several days ago, Hyun brought up some concerns about Clara to her manager, carefully describing the signs of Clara's drinking problem—a flushed facial skin, a strawberry nose, and a perpetually strong odor of alcohol whenever she spoke, even through a mask.

However, Hyun's manager shot her down. "She is going through tough times. You need to be more patient with her!"

"What about the safety of our patients?" Hyun asked.

"You just need to be an extra pair of eyes! Come on!" the manager barked at her.

Hyun left her manager's room feeling worse than before she'd talked to her.

Hyun noticed that Clara's nerves were getting the better of her. Hyun just hoped that she could get them under control before she made a mistake that would put Ginger in even more danger.

Clara checked Ginger's vitals and moved on to the IVs.

"I don't understand why it won't let me...dumb computer!" Clara muttered under her breath.

Hyun moved to her side to check the Medication Administration Record. "You need my signature for the Heparin since it's a high-risk medication," she said briskly.

Hyun went through the procedures, double-checking her patient's name, birth date, and ID number before co-signing for the medication. Of course, she knew the patient at this point, but it was adherence to the procedures that protected everyone. This was especially important now that they were all working twelve-hour shifts with overtime, constantly battling their own exhaustion.

Tom, the respiratory therapist, checked on the ventilator. He finished deep-suctioning Ginger and then administered DuoNeb. Five doctors were watching the proceedings and consulting Ginger's charts.

Dr. Lim was the cardiologist and Dr. Ortiz was the pulmonologist. Dr. Khan was a "hospitalist", the primary attending physician, so she often worked with Hyun. Joining them were Dr. Brown, a nephrologist, and Dr. Lee, an infectious disease specialist.

The ventilator suddenly began a high-pitched beeping.

"Can you deep-suction her again?" Dr. Khan asked Tom.

Tom's hands were steady even though his foot was ticking on the tile. Everyone in the room knew he was anxious to get out of there and take his next cigarette break. Still, he nodded.

"You bet. Her phlegm is still very thick. I'll give her albuterol afterward since I gave her DuoNeb a few minutes ago," he added as he quickly, but effectively, suctioned Ginger's airway by advancing the suction catheter down into the endotracheal tube, advancing it until it met the carina. He gently withdrew the catheter while applying suction. Then he flushed out the secretions into the canister from the suction catheter.

"The patient's troponin is still high, 5.4," Hyun announced to everyone in the room. "Her creatinine level is 5.5, BUN is out of whack, and the urine is badly saturated with poor output."

Dr. Brown stepped forward and assessed a urine Foley bag that hung at the side of the bed. The bag had only a few millimeters of dark, brown-colored urine, which had been collected during the last three hours. His face was calm, but his voice was shaking.

"Her kidneys are shutting down. We must dialyze her now."

Dr. Khan nodded, a pinched look on her face. "I received the patient's COVID-19 test result today, which only took five days compared to the typical seven days to two weeks. We got lucky this time. As we all suspected, she is positive for COVID. I've already informed the patient's brother, Daehan Kim, and his wife,

Mary. I really believe she will benefit from Actemra. Otherwise, I have no other options for her right now. Are we all in agreement on administering the Actemra for the patient?"

Upon getting nods from the specialists in the room, Dr. Khan continued, as if to reassure herself about the medication that she was about to have administered on Ginger. "Actemra is our last resort for her condition, but I've received some positive reports about this medication from other colleagues of mine. Dr. Lee and I already talked to the patient's brother about it. He is aware Actemra is usually used in RA to control inflammation. We explained to him that his sister's body is seriously inflamed. I told him Actemra could help to decrease the inflammation, especially in her lungs." She took a deep breath, and continued. "Right now, the best thing for this patient is to give her Actemra. Some of my colleagues have reported that it significantly decreased the inflammation of patients who were very sick and helped them recover. I believe Ginger is a perfect candidate for this medication. Daehan also understands that we don't have any other choice. This is a new disease for us and no one really knows the exact method of treatment. As all of you are aware, COVID-19 treatment is based on trial and error. We really don't have the magic wand, so I think we have to try the Actemra and hope for the best."

After a chorus of agreement, Dr. Khan went on more hesitantly. "I'll be blunt. Daehan Kim is pissed, and he has means at his disposal if things go wrong. If she dies, this could turn into a major lawsuit against the hospital where she works. We could easily get sucked into that mess. Regardless, lawsuit or no lawsuit, we have to do our very best to help this woman, and I believe this is our best bet."

Some voices spoke up with questions, but Dr. Khan waved them off. "There's no point in going into how and why Ginger Kim became ill."

Hyun listened carefully. *Ginger is Korean also?* She'd heard gossip about one of the administrators from another nurse who used to be employed by the Alderwood Medical Center, where Ginger had worked until she became ill. She didn't know if the allegations of racism and bullying were true, but based on her own experiences, it seemed plausible.

"I can't answer that right now," Dr. Khan insisted when Dr. Brown tried to press for answers. As the other doctors began filing out of the room, Dr. Khan turned back to Clara and Hyun. "Daehan and Mary asked to speak with the nurses, preferably through video chat, so I'll expect you to call them as soon as you finish what you're doing."

When Hyun nodded, Dr. Khan gave her a quick, pained smile, then glanced again at Ginger before leaving the room.

Clara let out an audible sigh of relief once the doctors had left.

"You shouldn't let them make you nervous," Hyun said softly.

"I can't help it. I feel like I'm on display."

We are, Hyun thought to herself. COVID was putting the entire medical community on display. All they could do was keep doing their job to the best of their ability.

When they had finished up, Hyun initiated the video call with Ginger's brother and sister-in-law. The couple's faces were pinched with worry as they appeared on screen.

"Good morning," Hyun said, smiling calmly.

"Good morning," they responded.

"My name is Hyun. I'm an RN here at the hospital. I've been an ECMO nurse for fifteen years and I'm working closely with your sister, Ginger."

"Is she awake?" Daehan asked anxiously.

"No."

"Can we see her?" Mary asked.

Hyun nodded. "Let me pass you to my colleague, Clara."

Clara took the phone and held it so they could see Ginger's face. After a few seconds, Clara said, "Now I'll put the phone near her ear so you can say hello."

Clara did, and Hyun listened to the heartbreak in Daehan's voice as he tried to reassure Ginger that everything was going to be okay. The truth was that none of them could actually make that promise, but it had to be said to keep everyone's hopes up. Hyun knew better than most that sometimes hope was the only measurable difference between a patient who lived and one who died.

When the couple finished saying what they wanted to say to Ginger, Hyun took the phone back.

"Would you like me to explain what we are doing for her?"

"Yes, please, in detail," Daehan said as Mary wiped away her tears and nodded.

Hyun turned the phone so they could see the ECMO machine.

"I'm going to give you some information about the devices so you can get more familiar with the equipment and how we are helping your sister. This is called the ECMO machine, which stands for extracorporeal membrane oxygenation. It's been around since 1970. This system helps rest your sister's heart and lungs by providing gas exchange outside of her body by this machine. One of the ECMO lines is inserted into her right femoral vein, and another is inserted into the left femoral artery."

She then pointed the camera over at the CRRT. "This is called continuous renal replacement therapy. It's basically hemodialysis on the ECMO machine to allow your sister's injured kidneys to rest while it takes over their function temporarily."

Daehan interrupted by asking again why his sister was on ECMO. It was too much for him to absorb and accept his sister's failing organs all at once.

Hyun explained to him again patiently, "It is because your sister's lungs and heart needed a break from overworking. We're trying to help prevent extreme damage from COVID-19."

"What about the ventilator? Does she still need that even though she is on ECMO?"

"Yes. The ventilator helps Ginger's lungs to oxygenate continuously, by mimicking her breathing motion."

"Is her heart still pumping even though ECMO took over her heart's circulatory system?" Mary asked this time.

"Yes, her heart still pumps. It should never stop."

"How did you plug those tubes into Ginger's groin?" Daehan asked, trying to calm himself down from all the overwhelming information about his dear baby sister.

"Excellent question. The access is surgically created by the surgeon. The surgeon will restore the vessels with stitches when she no longer needs the ECMO."

Hyun then went on to tell them what medications Ginger was on. She passed the phone briefly again to Clara, who showed them the IV medications and explained what they were all for.

"Do you have any other questions for me?" Hyun asked.

"Not at this time. Thank you for taking care of my sister," Daehan said somberly.

"You're very welcome."

After they hung up, they went back to work. As soon as Hyun completed the hemodialysis on Ginger, Clara administered the Actemra through the IV.

Hyun fervently hoped that the medication worked. Something had to. They needed something to fight the nightmare that was COVID-19. Things were only going to get worse for Ginger, and for them, as more patients flooded the hospital.

After administering the medication, Clara left the room quickly without saying a word to Hyun. Hyun was familiar with Clara's habit—hiding somewhere and smoking cigarettes.

Immediately after Clara exited the room, Hyun monitored Ginger for a possible side effect post-Actemra administration while monitoring her own ECMO machine. While re-checking Ginger's vitals, Hyun told Ginger, "I hope you're having pleasant dreams of somewhere far away from here."

Riyadh, Saudi Arabia
March 2002

Ginger woke up groggily. Several of the nurses she worked with at King Faisal Hospital had the flu. That meant more work and longer hours for the rest of the nurses.

She got up and quickly got ready for her day. As soon as she was done, she knocked on the door of her next-door neighbor. Dara opened the door a crack.

"How are you feeling?" Ginger asked.

"Terrible," Dara admitted. "Don't get this."

"I'll try not to," Ginger replied.

In truth, Ginger was using every safety precaution she could to avoid it. She said goodbye to Dara and went out into the hall of the nurses' dormitory. She looked up and down anxiously, waiting for a couple of the other nurses to walk over to the hospital with her. She waited for five minutes, but no one showed.

Finally, she walked to Rosa's room. Rosa had been on with her the day before, and she knew they shared the same schedule for the day. She knocked on the door and, after a moment, heard a raspy voice tell her to come in. She pushed open the door and saw Rosa sitting on her bed, her face scarlet, her nose swollen, and a wad of tissues clutched in her hand.

"You got it too?" Ginger asked.

Rosa nodded miserably. "How come you never get sick?" she asked.

Ginger just shrugged. "Lucky, I guess." She didn't mention that it had more to do with care and preparation than luck.

"I'm sorry," Rosa said. "I know this means more work for you."

"It's okay," Ginger said. "Is the new girl working today?"

Rosa shook her head. "She's worse than I am."

"Oh," said Ginger, feeling a little more anxious at the thought of walking by herself. "Do you know who else is on with us?"

"No. Oh! You're not thinking of walking over by yourself, are you?"

Ginger winced and said, "I don't really have much of a choice."

After all, she wasn't sick, so she really couldn't miss work. She especially couldn't miss it given that they were short-staffed at the moment.

"Oh, you can't. Maybe I can pull myself together," Rosa said, trying to stand up from the bed. She got up, wobbled for a second, then started to cough uncontrollably.

"Oh my goodness! You need to take care of yourself. Hydrate yourself with water or tea, and get plenty of rest, Rosa. I'll be okay. It's broad daylight and I'll walk fast," Ginger said, trying to reassure her.

"That doesn't matter," Rosa said. "They took my cousin Queenie. I warned her, but she wouldn't listen." Tears glistened in her feverish eyes.

"It's okay, I've got this," Ginger said, pulling a small bottle out of her purse.

"What is that?"

"Mace. My brother, Daehan, sent it from America six months ago. Apparently, all I have to do is spray it in someone's eyes when you are attacked by a stranger."

"Can your brother send me some?"

"I will see."

"Be careful," Rosa said.

"I will."

"Make sure you walk back tonight with someone."

"I will."

"And let me know when you're back here," Rosa implored.

"I will. I promise, I'll be fine," Ginger said. She gave Rosa a smile that she hoped was reassuring. She left the room, closing the door behind her.

In the corridor, Ginger straightened her shoulders and took several deep breaths. She decided to hold the mace in her hand so it would be ready when she needed it.

If I need it, she told herself, hoping things wouldn't come to that.

When Ginger marched outside, the arid desert air hit her full blast. She had never become accustomed to just how dry it was in Saudi Arabia. She clutched the mace so tightly in her fist, her fingers ached.

She hurried on her way, moving her eyes back and forth. She had been in Saudi Arabia for three years, but there was still so much she had yet to adjust to. It was more than just the physical climate, it was the social one as well. She'd worked as a nurse for five years back home before she'd gotten the desire to see more of the world and accepted the nursing contract in Saudi Arabia.

She'd thought that the discrimination against women in South Korea had been terrible. But she hadn't truly understood just how bad things could be for women until she had moved here.

The hospital was like its own special environment, populated with doctors and nurses from many different countries. It was a cutting-edge facility that did a lot of research, on top of everything else. Still, stepping foot outside it was taking her life in her own hands. From day one, the hospital staff had drilled into the nurses that they should never walk alone, even from their dorm to the hospital. Many nurses had been kidnapped, never to be seen again.

The years she spent as a child learning about the dangers of the world had made her more cautious than most. This was her first time walking by herself in three years, and she could feel her heart pounding as she struggled to keep hold of the mace despite her sweaty hands.

Had she been at the hospital with no one to walk home with, she would have waited for hours if she had to. But she couldn't wait now, not without being late for her shift.

She saw several local women, all covered from head to toe, each heading intently to where they needed to be. She saw one man, but he was busy talking to a child who was walking beside him.

When she made it to the hospital, Ginger finally breathed a sigh of relief. She put away her mace and pulled herself together. There were patients who needed her help and she needed to look calm, strong, and confident when they saw her.

As Ginger emerged into the corridor, she ran into her supervisor, who smiled at her. The woman handed her an envelope.

"You got some mail," she said to Ginger.

Ginger took it, noticed it was from her brother, and put it in her purse to read later.

"Thank you."

"You're welcome. I'd like to make an appointment to talk to you next week about your plans."

"My plans?" Ginger asked, still struggling to refocus her mind.

"Your original contract with the hospital is up next month, so I want to discuss whether you intend to stay on."

"Oh, yes. Let's meet Monday at ten."

"Great, see you then." Her supervisor nodded and moved on.

Ginger took a deep breath as she weighed her options. After a moment, she decided it was better to think things through later when she had more time. For the moment, she had rounds to do.

When her shift was finally over, Ginger found another girl, Julia, to walk back with her to the dorms. Julia had only been there for about six months, but she was dating one of the doctors and was considering what it would be like if she settled in Saudi Arabia permanently.

"He doesn't want to work somewhere else?" Ginger asked, feeling more relaxed than she had been on her morning walk.

"No, he is one of the researchers. This is his dream job," Julia replied without hesitation.

"What is your dream job?" Ginger asked.

"To be a doctor's wife," Julia said with a giggle.

Ginger smiled, thinking of her friend Eungi back home. Eungi had married a handsome doctor right before Ginger left for Saudi Arabia. They'd just had their first child, and Eungi had sent pictures in her last letter.

"Well, it sounds like you might just get it!"

"I'm pretty sure he's going to propose tomorrow night. He's taking me out to dinner at this really fancy restaurant."

"Congratulations!"

"We'll have a big wedding, and all my family—"

Suddenly, Ginger felt a hand grab her arm. It spun her halfway around as she heard Julia scream in terror. A man was leering down at Ginger, and out of the corner of her eye, she could see a second one pick Julia up and move toward a waiting car.

"Help!" Ginger screamed at the top of her lungs. She fumbled in her purse, and her hand wrapped around the mace. She yanked it out, depressed it, and the first shot went wild, missing the man who picked her up.

She brought her arm around and got her hand right up next to his eyes before shooting the mace at him again. This time, the liquid hit him full in the face. He screamed and dropped her to the ground. Ginger fell, ripping her scrubs as she hit the pavement. She scrambled to her feet and ran as he clawed at his eyes and swore at her.

She turned to look for Julia and saw the car that she had just been pushed into speed away. Ginger glanced again at the man she had sprayed and then ran for the dormitory. Her heart was pounding so loudly in her ears, she couldn't hear whether he was chasing her or not. She pushed herself faster, pain shooting through her knee, which she must have twisted when she'd fallen.

Ginger finally made it to the building, punched in the security code with her shaking hand, yanked open the door, then slammed it closed. She ran to her room, threw herself inside, locked it, and then sat down on her bed, shuddering.

The mace she had still been holding onto fell out of her hand and rolled under her bed, but she didn't bother retrieving it. Instead, she put her head on her knees and sobbed.

Julia was gone, and all her hopes and dreams with her. There was no use calling the police. No one would be able to find her, even if they bothered trying—which they wouldn't. Men made the laws here and women were property, nothing more. Women had no rights.

After several minutes, she forced herself to get up. She needed to talk to Rosa about Julia.

She found Rosa still sick, looking slightly worse than she had that morning. Rosa was devastated when Ginger told her about Julia, and her grief caused Ginger to start crying again.

"It's this terrible place!" Rosa yelled, her hoarse voice full of sadness and anger. "How are we supposed to live like this?"

"We should tell someone!"

"Who? The police don't care. It's just a woman who's been kidnapped," Rosa said. "I know, I've been through this before."

"I know the police won't help us, but what about the hospital? They hired her. Julia is their employee," Ginger argued.

"I tried that last time. You know what they did? They shrugged their shoulders and told me she'd been warned. That was it. Then they hired someone else. Queenie didn't matter to them. She was just a body to fill a need. One woman is as good as another, as far as they're concerned, and if they lose some, oh well. Julia doesn't matter to them. *We* don't matter to them."

It wasn't right. The injustice of it burned inside Ginger. She thought of all the Saudi women she saw on the streets and in the hospital. They were oppressed, bullied, and had no rights. Men made every decision for them, to the point where their lives were no different than those of slaves.

And there's nothing I can do about it, she thought in despair.

Ginger could feel herself beginning to shake. Suddenly, she felt like she was back in her parents' home, cowering in the corner of the family room and praying that the soldiers wouldn't come to kill her and her family, or take them all away.

Like Julia had been taken away.

Only Ginger knew in her heart that Julia hadn't been taken to a prison, not in the same sense. She knew that Julia would be used, abused, and tortured. If she died quickly, it would probably be a blessing. It was terrible to think that way, but the dark future that Julia faced under the hands of her captors would be too cruel for her to bear.

Ginger remembered a conversation that she had shared with a Korean journalist at the airport three years earlier, when she was waiting for the plane to Saudi Arabia. He told Ginger to "be careful" and shared his experience about meeting a blind Korean nurse.

"I got lost in the desert," he recounted. "It was purely by chance. I met her in one of the nomads' tents." He learned that the nurse had been kidnapped by two men when she lost her co-workers in the crowd at the outdoor market in Saudi Arabia. She had been blindfolded, bounded, and gagged after she was shoved into the taxicab.

The reporter described with an even more somber tone of voice, "The Korean nurse was sold twice. They even gouged her eyes out so she wouldn't run away. She was almost half-dead when she was finally 'purchased' by the nomad—her current husband. She was raped repeatedly, to the point where she had given up hope and stopped running away. She told me, 'Being blind, I have nowhere to run to in this desert.'"

The reporter continued on, "I offered to help her escape, but she declined, saying, 'There is no place for me in Korea anymore. I do not want my family to see me like this and find out about my torture, especially my parents. It will be too much for them to handle. Besides, I do not want to be their burden. I'd rather continue living my life here with my two daughters.'"

At the time, Ginger didn't know what to think about his horrific tale. For all she knew, it could have simply been a made-up story by a bored reporter while waiting for his plane. But after witnessing Julia's kidnapping and hearing Rosa's story about her cousin Queenie, Ginger realized that it wasn't just a tall tale.

There is some truth to the horrible story.

Ginger balled her hands into fists and couldn't stop the hot tears from running down her cheeks. She wept for Julia and the blind nurse—both of their lives had been completely destroyed overnight.

I can't believe that this happened in the 20th century, let alone the fact that it's happening in the 21st century.

It was as true now as it had been when she was a child, huddled in the dark while her brother fought for their rights, for their voice to be heard. There had been nothing she could do to help back then. And even though she was a grown woman now and not a scared little girl, there was still nothing she could do to help.

That realization pierced her to her core. She stared at Rosa, who was openly weeping.

Rosa was broken. She had tried to stand up before, and she had been smacked down. It was clear that she wouldn't fight back anymore.

Ginger stood up abruptly and went back to her room. She pulled the letter from her brother out of her purse. Through her tears, she read it three times.

Daehan was encouraging her to move to America. Apparently, they had a need for good nurses. He had mentioned this need before, but this time there was an urgency in his writing.

Or maybe the urgency she felt was deep inside herself. She sat for a while, head bowed over the letter, thinking and praying for guidance.

In the dark hours before dawn, everything became clear. She would go to America, where things *had* to be better. She was just so tired of working in this hospital. It was a place of healing, but she couldn't stop fearing for her life.

CHAPTER 7

Seattle, Washington
March 17, 2020

Hyun hated having to work for fear of losing her life. She was standing in the ICU room, staring down at Ginger.

Next to her, Clara raised her hand to scratch her nose. She'd been wearing the same N95 mask for five days. Hyun had strong doubts about how much protection the mask was offering at that point, but it was better than nothing.

All the ICU nurses had been wearing washable, yellow isolation gowns throughout their twelve-hour shifts. They'd all had to become creative rule-breakers since the beginning of the pandemic. When they got a bite to eat or used the restroom, they'd each hang their yellow gown over a hand sanitizer dispenser. They had to reuse the one gown throughout their twelve-hour shift.

Hyun was faring slightly better than the rest of them. She had a respirator and the eye shield. Still, she felt exposed and hated the fact that they couldn't use fresh gowns throughout the day.

Hyun was also concerned about the hospital-wide cross-contamination when she saw other nurses caring for two or three ICU patients—one COVID-confirmed, the others COVID rule-out patients. It was entirely unlike the ICU's one to one, two to one, or three to one patient/nurse ratio. She predicted that the problem would be worse in the Progressive Care Unit, Med/ Surg, and ED since those departments' patient and nurse ratio was either four to one or five to one—sometimes even six to one. Since the start of the pandemic, all the written hospital policies and regulations had been thrown out the window.

This is madness, Hyun thought.

As usual, the medical team was once again gathered around Ginger Kim as the doctors consulted their notes. They were talking amongst themselves when Dr. Lee suddenly addressed Hyun.

"Where did you get that respirator and the eye shield?"

"I wish I had one so I could use it with extra filters," Tom said, his frustration heavy in his voice. "I asked my manager for a new N95, but he said he doesn't have any. I really need one like that."

Clara was nodding and scowling in agreement. "Me too. It's not like I want to die. I'd pay for it, even."

Hyun looked around the room. She had a limited supply, but she knew she had to help. "I'll give each of you one. No need to pay."

"How is the patient?" Dr. Khan asked, interrupting.

"Her heart rate is still in the 130s, sinus tachycardia," Clara responded.

Dr. Khan nodded. "I reviewed her last 24-hour vital signs. Sometimes her heart rate dipped down to the 120s for a few seconds, but it would shoot right back up to the 130s. Her blood gas also is still up there. Can you collect the set of new vitals now?"

"VS, BP 88/50, heart rate 130 with sinus rhythm, respiration vent, temp 101, oxygen 100% vent," Clara reported.

"She needs more IV fluid and Tylenol. I'll type the orders now. When was her last IV Tylenol?" Dr. Khan asked as she typed in the orders.

"It was six hours ago."

The ventilator began beeping. Tom quickly but effectively suctioned Ginger's airway. "The phlegm in her airway is still very thick, but I don't want to suction her too aggressively because of the safety concerns, I'll give her a break and suction her again later. All my COVID patients have a large amount of thick phlegm and it plugs up their airway."

"It's a common problem we see in all the COVID patients, and it is killing them because it obstructs their airway." Dr. Khan agreed. She gazed at Ginger and sighed. "Her condition hasn't improved at all."

Dr. Lee responded, "Her body has been in shock for too long Let's keep it up. Time will tell."

"We can't lose her," Dr. Khan said. She turned to Tom, "Would you give her another DuoNeb now?"

"Of course."

Hyun continued about her duties, but worry was gnawing at her. Pretty soon, there wouldn't be any eye shields, respirators, or masks. What would they do then? They'd be completely exposed to the virus. How could they heal the sick when just being near them would cause all the nurses and doctors to join their ranks?

Glancing again at Ginger's face, Hyun wondered how Ginger had contracted COVID-19. It had very likely happened on the job, caring for her patients without sufficient PPE. Hyun was suddenly overwhelmed by the thought that it could be her next, lying there unconscious, completely overtaken by the virus. That reality, combined with the swiftly evaporating self-supplied non-hospital-grade protective equipment, filled her with dread. She felt helpless. Even worse, she felt trapped.

Anchorage, Alaska
June 2002

Ginger felt free. In some ways, it felt like she was free for the first time in her life. She took a deep breath of crisp, clean air. She was driving on the Seward Highway in her Jeep, and she felt like she was on top of the world.

Alaska was beautiful. She'd fallen in love with its pristine landscape and its wonderful air. It was a sunny day, and with the breeze blowing against her face, she couldn't remember the last time she'd felt so happy.

What a contrast.

She hadn't realized just how oppressive it had been in Saudi Arabia until she'd made it to Alaska. Her brother had been right—America was the place to be. She wished she lived closer to him, but at least they were on the same continent now.

Ginger could now do so many things she hadn't been able to do in Saudi Arabia. Driving was quickly becoming a favorite activity of hers. She loved the freedom it brought. Of course, just being able to walk safely down the street by herself was a relief. Even though she knew she was safe, she still kept her mace in her purse just in case. She thought that no matter how safe she was, the old fears and habits would never leave her.

As she stared at the breathtaking scenery of the Turnagain Arm, unwanted images flashed in her mind. She couldn't help but compare the peace and serenity around her with the chaos and blood of the Gwangju massacre. Her heart began to pound a little faster, as it always did when those memories surfaced.

She breathed slowly and deeply, pushing them back down. She reminded herself that she was in a safe place now. She was here in the land of democracy. She had what her family and friends had fought and died for—freedom. She thought of Misoon and Yeoni who had been shot and killed.

It could have been me.

"I must live life to its fullest, for me and for those who were killed," Ginger said firmly to herself, a promise to herself and the beauty surrounding her.

Ginger finally made it to work. Angels Medical Center was one of the largest hospitals in the state. It professed to be a Catholic non-profit hospital, so when signing her two-year contract, she had thought the medical institution would put the patients' needs before anything and everything.

The serenity of the landscape outside was in stark contrast with the frantic activity inside the hospital. Ginger sat and waited for the assignment sheet from the PCU charge nurse along with Mika, a Japanese nurse who had been working there for over a year, and Emily, a Caucasian nurse who had been there for roughly the same amount of time.

The harried-looking charge nurse quickly passed out the assignment sheets.

"Excuse me," Ginger said as she looked over the sheet.

"Problem?" the charge nurse asked, raising her eyebrow.

"I have twice as many patients as Emily, and so does Mika."

"So?" the charge nurse asked, eyes narrowing.

"So I think there's been a mistake. It's going to be hard to handle that many patients, especially with three high-acuity patients. Maybe Emily can take one more."

"Emily has the appropriate amount," the charge nurse said dismissively.

Ginger glanced at Emily, who looked away quickly.

"How is this possible?"

"Do you have a hearing problem or an attitude problem?" the charge nurse snapped.

Ginger was taken aback.

"Neither. She's fine, and so am I," Mika spoke up before Ginger could say anything else.

"Good," the charge nurse snapped before walking away. She was followed by Emily, who looked like a puppy following its master.

"I don't understand. Is Emily having trouble keeping up?" Ginger asked. It was the first time she'd been on a shift with Emily.

"You really don't understand," Mika said with a short, bitter laugh.

"What do you mean?" Ginger asked.

Mika looked around, then pulled Ginger toward a supply room.

"Emily gets less work than us because she's white."

"That doesn't make any sense," Ginger said, still confused.

"No, it doesn't. Those of us who aren't white are expected to do more, end up with more seriously-ill patients, and take it all without asking questions."

"That can't be right," Ginger objected. "You must be mistaken."

Mika laughed again. "I've worked here for over a year. Trust me, I know what I'm talking about. You're new. You've only been on shifts mainly with women like us, so you haven't had a chance to notice."

"But the hospital is understaffed. Everyone should be pulling their weight," Ginger protested.

"They should, but they don't. In this place, being white equals less work and easier work."

In Saudi Arabia, Ginger had worked with nurses from dozens of countries of many different ethnicities, but preference had never been given to one over another.

"We need to tell the administration!"

Mika looked at Ginger like she was crazy. "You think they don't know?"

"How can they let this go on?" Ginger asked.

"It's all about preserving the status quo. It will be that way until everyone stands up to them," replied Mika in a rather detached tone of voice.

"Why don't they?"

"No one wants to get fired. No one wants to be the first."

CHAPTER 8

Seattle, Washington
March 18, 2020

"One of the first celebrities to get the disease, Tom Hanks, was discharged a couple of days ago along with his wife, Rita, from a hospital in Australia. The couple is doing well and quarantining at home," the news anchor on the TV announced. "Yesterday was the first St. Patrick's Day in recent history that was somber, with more people wearing black than green as the death toll continues to climb. Stocks are struggling to rebound from the worst day on the market since 1987."

Hyun turned off the television in Ginger's room. The news was getting harder to watch as the corona-related death numbers became more terrifying.

"My sister in Northern California said that they were just told to shelter in place," Clara said grimly. "It's spreading rapidly there."

"I hope she'll be alright," Hyun said sympathetically, trying not to let herself worry about her own friends and family. The only people she could help at this point were those in this hospital. Worrying wasn't doing them or her any good.

Together, they worked to turn Ginger and check her skin. Everything was looking the same as it did yesterday, which was a blessing for all of them.

"This bed is doing a good job!" Hyun was thrilled. "The automated massaging function is really working well! I don't see a single bedsore!"

"I love when things work the way they're supposed to," Clara remarked.

"You can say that again. At least we witnessed one positive thing in Ginger's condition today. I have some hope for her!"

Hyun was serious. It was a slim hope, but it was something. At least, nothing else was going wrong for the moment. Sometimes that was all you could ask for in life.

Ginger's brother requested another video call. Hyun activated it and didn't have to struggle as she put a smile on her face.

Daehan must have noticed her expression because he instantly asked, "Is she better?"

"Not yet, but she isn't worse either. Sometimes that's a blessing in and of itself."

He looked crestfallen, but managed to nod in agreement. "I wish I could visit her…see her in person."

"I know, but it's safer this way. For you and for her."

For all of us.

It didn't matter what Hyun said. Even if Daehan tried to come to the hospital, they would stop him at the front door. All elective surgeries had been canceled for the foreseeable future, and visitors were now forbidden. She understood the reasons why, but her heart broke for the families who couldn't see their loved ones, particularly when it would be their last opportunity to do so. She reminded herself to keep smiling, even if sadness kept creeping into her thoughts.

"Would you like to see her?" Hyun asked.

Daehan nodded.

She put the phone near Ginger and tried not to listen too closely as Daehan spoke a few words to her. She couldn't offer him privacy, but she tried not to pry. Finally, he called for Hyun, and she faced the phone so she could see Daehan and discuss Ginger's care.

"How long do you think she's going to be in the hospital?" he asked, his voice choked up.

"I wish I knew," she answered truthfully.

She didn't tell him that given how little they knew of the disease, even if Ginger did wake up, they wouldn't be able to discharge her anytime soon.

Anchorage, Alaska
March 2004

"No! You cannot discharge my patient!" Ginger said heatedly. "You're risking his life if you do."

She was staring down Emily, who had become one of the discharge nurses at the hospital. Emily was standing with her hands on her hips, eyes blazing angrily as she stared back at Ginger.

"Who do you think you are?" Emily spat out.

"I'm Mr. Hill's primary nurse. I will not sign off on him leaving this hospital while knowing he is not safe to be discharged. You should ask the doctor to write a transfer order to the Med/Surg instead," Ginger told Emily.

"Nope, I'm not going to! Look, he can call 911 if he has a problem."

"Not if he's unconscious!"

"He's on my list. I'm getting him out of here today."

"You know what you can do with your 'Kill List'?"

"Look, the hospital only has so many beds. We need to free them up as soon as we can."

"I've seen your post-discharge plan. It's ridiculous. This man needs continued medical attention, not a handful of painkillers," Ginger continued to argue.

It was not the first time she'd had such an argument with one of the discharge nurses. The discharge nurses' sole purpose was to clear beds to get in more patients, thereby making more profit for the supposedly non-profit hospital. To that end, they discharged many patients who were still in need of care.

It was dangerous and flew in the face of everything Ginger believed. In her mind, sending home patients, knowing that discharging them early could hurt or even kill them, was tantamount to murder.

But she was the only one yelling about it. She didn't know why more nurses didn't stand up to the unethical and unsafe practice. Even the doctors often caved to the demands of the discharge nurses.

"I won't sign," Ginger said, folding her arms across her chest.

"Then I'll just find someone who will," Emily said with a smirk. "Don't worry, Florence Nightingale, your reputation for standing in the way of hospital policy won't be tarnished."

Before Ginger could say anything, Emily stormed away with her head held high. Ginger let out a sigh and shook her head.

She took a deep breath and stepped back into Mr. Hill's room. The older man smiled wanly when he saw her.

"How are you this morning, Mr. Hill?" she asked, hating that there was a catch in her voice.

"Better, now that you're here," he said slowly, wheezing slightly. "You always take such good care of me."

"I bet you say that to all the pretty nurses," she said, trying to keep her tone light even though she wanted to scream.

"No, I don't say things lightly. Besides, I figure since I see you everywhere, you must be my own personal nurse. A guardian angel sent by my Agnes to watch out for me."

Ginger had been a float nurse for a while, floating between the ED, PCU, and occasionally, the ICU. This was the third day in a row she'd seen Mr. Hill. She could see why he was starting to think she was his personal nurse. But she certainly wasn't his guardian angel, not unless she could find a way to keep Emily from discharging him early.

She turned her head away so he wouldn't see the frustrated expression on her face. She wanted to see him get well. She was afraid if they discharged him now, he'd be right back in the ED within 24 hours. Of course, that was the best-case scenario. He could also end up dead.

Ginger kept up a light chatter while she took care of him. When she finally finished, Ginger gave him a bright smile before leaving the room. She had a list of patients she still had to see, but first, she needed a few moments to herself to get her emotions under control.

She headed down a hallway in the PCU. There, sitting by herself on the floor, was one of the newer nurses. Maria was a Mexican-American nurse who often confided in Ginger about the discrimination she experienced at the hospital. As Ginger got closer, she could hear Maria sobbing.

Ginger knelt down beside her and put her hand over Maria's shoulder lightly so as not to startle her. Maria's shoulders only shook harder.

"Was it Dr. Cox?" Ginger asked.

Maria's jerky nod confirmed her guess, and Ginger tugged her into a nearby restroom, where she handed Maria some paper towels and waited on the latest outrage. Dr. Cox was a bully of an ENT surgeon—a short, stocky, middle-aged man who loved to flirt with the Caucasian nurses. Especially blondes.

Maria finally calmed down enough to speak, then she exploded. "He threw a fit about the wrong type of trach tube placed in the patient's bedside." She began imitating him, "'What IS this? Where is the non-cuffed trach he's supposed to have at the bedside? Huh? He shouldn't be using this! Are you trying to kill my patient?'"

Ginger let out a long sigh and contemplated what to say to Maria. As always, Dr. Cox was way out of line, not only overreacting but also unprofessional. He hadn't given Maria a chance to explain the situation.

"It's so unfair!" Maria continued, tears streaming from her face. "Dr. Cox was the one who made a mistake by not ordering the correct type of trach!"

Besides that, Ginger thought, Dr. Cox and the RT were equally responsible for obtaining the right trach tube, just as much as the primary nurse. But mentioning that wouldn't help now.

Reaching out, Ginger hugged Maria, "I'm here if you need to talk, Maria. You know I've been thrown under the bus like this before."

There wasn't anything else to be said. By the time Maria calmed down, they'd both run out of their meager break time, so they parted ways and promised to keep supporting each other. Both of them knew all too well that neither the charge nurse nor the manager would bother sticking up for Maria.

Throughout the rest of her morning rounds, Ginger thought about how she could help Mr. Hill and Maria. There had to be something she could do. They both needed someone to stand up for them.

Ginger had so many patients to visit that she was almost two hours late in taking her lunch break. After she finally completed her morning round on all her patients, she made up her mind to fight for both Mr. Hill and Maria, right up to the director of the hospital if that was what it took.

She decided to pop in and see Mr. Hill on her way to the cafeteria to grab a bite to eat. Her stomach rumbled angrily, but she told herself the delay would only cost her a minute or two.

"Good afternoon, Mr. Hill," she said as she pushed open the door to his room and walked inside. She froze in mid-stride. His bed was empty, with the sheets rumpled. She checked the bathroom. He wasn't there. Finally, with a sinking heart, she checked the closet. His belongings were gone as well.

Ginger thought that Emily might have had him discharged, so she had to find Emily quickly.

Just then, she heard hysterical shouting in the hall outside. She raced out of the room and headed for the nurses' station, which seemed to be the source of the shouting.

When she reached the station, she found Maria standing there, clutching a stack of papers in her hand, screaming at Emily and the house supervisor.

"You agreed to sign it," Emily said mildly when Maria paused for a moment.

"How could I not with you threatening me?" Maria demanded. "I've had it! I've had it with you and this fucked-up place. Non-profit? That's a joke. Everything this hospital does is about making money, not healing people. As far as I'm concerned, you're all a bunch of murderers. Well, I'm done. I'm done with being picked on and yelled at for no good reason. You can all go straight to hell and take this with you!"

With that, Maria threw the papers at Emily's face and walked off. All the paper flew up above Emily's head, then landed on the floor, some on Emily's shoes. Emily shook her feet and stepped back, dislodging the papers and scattering them all over the floor.

"No one in Alaska will hire her after that," the supervisor said, shaking her head.

Ginger knew the woman meant it. She'd had nurses blacklisted for less.

"Foreigners are always so unstable!" Emily said, her laugh a bit shaky. She looked down at the papers scattered all over the floor. "What a mess."

Emily glanced up and her eyes locked onto Ginger. A cruel smile spread across her face.

"Oh, Ginger, be a dear and pick that up," she said, turning to walk down the hall with the supervisor who was still muttering about Maria.

Ginger wanted to shout that she refused to do so, but by the time she found her voice, both women had turned the corner. She turned to look at the other nurses. The Japanese nurse and the

Filipino nurse both dropped their eyes. The white nurse just stared insolently at her, as though waiting, *wanting*, to see Ginger kneel down and pick up the papers.

She didn't want to, but the papers scattered all over the floor were part of a patient's file. A confidential file. It couldn't be left that way.

She knelt down, choking on her own anger as she did so. She quickly began shuffling the papers back into the folder. Then, the name of a patient caught her eye—James Hill. She could also see Maria's signature underneath his, and realized what had become the final straw for Maria.

Emily had forced Maria to help her send Mr. Hill home because Ginger disagreed with her. Ginger was so disappointed, she felt as if all the energy had been sucked out of her body. Both people she had vowed to fight for were now gone, and there was nothing she could do for either of them.

CHAPTER 9

Seattle, Washington
March 19, 2020

"I quit!"

Hyun froze, her hand on the door to Ginger's room. The words rang out all along the hallway of the nurses' station.

She slowly turned, looking at the nurses' station. The usually noisy hallway became unnaturally hushed as though everyone and everything were waiting to hear the words that came next.

"What did you say?" Hyun recognized the second voice as belonging to Susan, the nursing director.

As if compelled, Hyun walked forward until she could see the first speaker. It was Matthew, an RN who was just getting off his shift. He and Joe were the night team that took care of Ginger.

"You heard me," Matthew said. "If I can't wear protective gear, then I quit."

In his hands, he was holding one of the respirators and the eye shield that Hyun had given out. She winced. She had none left, as she'd shared all she could. The respirators with shields had actually come from her husband, who had a house-painting business. Since his business had shut down due to COVID, he'd let her take them to work because the hospital couldn't—or *wouldn't*—provide them.

Susan stood, ramrod straight, her short blonde hair perfect with not a strand out of place. Her makeup was elaborately styled for all the world to see. Since the start of this whole nightmare, she had chosen to not wear a mask. Hyun had overheard Susan tell one of the other administrators that she was "setting an example" for the nursing staff.

"You cannot wear any PPE not approved by the hospital," Susan said crisply.

"Great, then have the hospital give me protective equipment and I'll use that," Matthew replied.

"There is no need for these!" Susan snatched the respirator and the eye shield out of Matthew's hand.

Clara had appeared from the other direction, wearing her own respirator and the eye shield that had also been supplied by Hyun. She gawked at the sight of Susan with Matthew's respirator and the eye shield in her hand.

Susan focused her attention on Clara, she then glanced at Hyun.

"The two of you are breaking hospital policy and I should fire you both," Susan snapped.

Clara hastily took off her respirator and the eye shield and put them on the counter next to the computer where she usually sat for charting. "Hyun gave them to me. I didn't want to wear them, but I was trying not to hurt her feelings," she lied.

Hyun gasped in disbelief and wondered how Clara could do that to her.

"So you're the troublemaker. I should have known," Susan said to Hyun. "Take off that respirator and the eye shield!"

"No, I can't," Hyun replied quietly. "I need it to protect myself."

"I ordered you to take them off!"

"I can't, because it's unsafe," Hyun responded more firmly this time as felt her heart pound faster.

"Take them off or lose your job," Susan threatened.

Hyun took a deep breath. "If the hospital provides sufficient PPE, I will not wear my own. Until then, I must wear these. I know my job is to take care of the patients, but I don't want to die. I have two little kids and a husband who I have to look after."

"Is that all you have to say?" Susan asked as she glared at Hyun.

"One more thing," Hyun replied. "I'll make sure you get fired before you fire me!"

Susan glared at her for a moment, then looked around at the ICU nurses surrounding her. She threw Matthew's respirator and the eye shield on the counter, where they bounced off and landed right next to Clara's respirator. She angrily turned and marched off without a word. Her high heels clicked down the corridor and could be heard for several seconds after she had disappeared from sight.

"What the hell was that?" Joe, the night ECMO RN, asked in bewilderment.

Hyun just shook her head, at a loss for words.

Clara refused to look at her. Instead, she turned to Matthew. "You're not really quitting, are you?" she asked, wide-eyed.

Matthew grumbled something under his breath, picked up his respirator and the eye shield, then walked off. Clara also picked up her respirator that she'd abandoned on the counter.

Hyun lingered at the nurses' station for a few more minutes, discussing Ginger's status with Joe. She wasn't sure how she was supposed to work side by side with Clara after she'd thrown her under the bus. Clara's work performance was poor to begin with, and Hyun had caught more than a few of her mistakes. Now Hyun knew that Clara would lie and betray her at the slightest provocation, and that was unnerving. When Hyun was focusing all her efforts on patient care, how was she expected to watch her back at the same time?

Hyun made her way back to Ginger's room, and several minutes later, Clara joined her. Clara did not offer a single word of explanation or apology. She was wearing her respirator with the shield on, her face hidden behind her gear. Hyun just shook her head and focused on her job so her frustration wouldn't interfere with Ginger's care.

The doctors all shuffled together into the room, beginning the daily ritual of evaluating and deciding on Ginger's care.

"It's four days post-Actemra administration and there hasn't been much improvement," Hyun informed the doctors. "I think we might need to dialyze her again. Her BUN is still unstable, and she only put out 100cc of saturated urine for the past six hours."

Clara spoke up. "Fortunately, her troponin level is decreasing. It's down to 5 from 5.4. Her temp is now 99 degrees, and her heart rate is down to the 120s with sinus tachycardia."

Dr. Khan and Dr. Lim nodded in agreement.

"I agree. She needs to be dialyzed again," Dr. Brown said. "Let's do that now. I'll type up the orders."

"I'm cautiously optimistic," Dr. Khan remarked after taking a look at Ginger.

Hyun and Clara finished their tasks on administering the am medication after the doctors left. Hyun surreptitiously checked everything Clara was doing. When Clara was getting ready to go out for her smoke break, she turned on the news and stared at the TV, seemingly transfixed as the news announcers cited the latest death tolls from around the world.

After Clara left the room, Hyun meticulously rechecked the ECMO machine and its access sites on Ginger's groin, on both her right and left. The sites were patent—that is, without any signs of infection. She then assessed Ginger from head to toe and glanced sympathetically down at her.

"Things are very crazy around here," she said softly to Ginger. "I hope all the bad news doesn't stress you out."

Anchorage, Alaska
June 2004

Ginger was feeling a bit melancholy as she moved through her new night shift. She'd received a letter that morning from her friend Eungi. There were more pictures of Eungi and her family. But instead of making her feel closer to her friend, it made her seem farther away.

Ginger was feeling isolated, alone. Because of the shifts she was working, phone calls were out of the question. Therefore, communication with her best friend had been relegated to a few scribbled words on a piece of paper.

Ginger was friendly with some of the nurses she worked with, but she didn't have any real, close friends in Anchorage. That made everything harder.

When her break came, she stopped by the nurses' station,

where some of the others were engaging in small talk—some of it medical, some of it personal. Ginger thought it might be a good opportunity for her to engage in a quick friendly conversation with them.

"I got a rare diagnosis," Ginger said, figuring they would all find it interesting. "My dentist and the oral surgeon told me that I have to remove one of my teeth because my body is attacking it. Can you imagine? My immune system is attacking one of my own teeth."

"Oh, yuck! Disgusting! What is wrong with you? Why would you share that?" Barb asked, scowling at her.

"What? It's interesting. Apparently, it's pretty uncommon."

"We don't want to see your gross tooth."

Ginger stared at her in surprise. "What's wrong with you? Do you even know what I'm talking about? My tooth looks completely normal to the naked eye. Why are you judging me and assuming that my tooth is gross? You're a nurse. How do you empty out your patients' commodes or bedpans?"

Barb turned red in the face and stormed away in a huff.

"You're in trouble now. She's heading for the supervisor's office," one of the other nurses said with a smirk.

"Why?" Ginger questioned.

The other nurses just shook their heads.

Several hours later, Ginger was still replaying the whole incident in her mind as she drove home. She'd been called into the supervisor's office at the end of her shift and was asked to apologize to Barb for being rude. She'd told the supervisor that she wouldn't apologize since she had nothing to apologize for. She was sure it hadn't earned her any popularity points, but she wouldn't pretend that she had been the problem in that conversation.

Unfortunately, it hadn't been the most disturbing thing to happen to her that night. She'd witnessed a Final Pray, and she couldn't get it out of her head. She had just stood and watched throughout, feeling helpless.

That, combined with the isolation she'd already been feeling, had brought her right back to hiding in her home, unable to talk to Eungi. She wanted to call Eungi when she got home, but the time difference made that impractical.

When she was thirteen, she wouldn't have cared. She would have called anyway.

After making it home and taking a shower, Ginger decided to write her feelings down as if she were talking to Eungi.

Eungi,

I witnessed a "Final Pray" during my shift last night in PCU. This ended up being the last straw for me in terms of AMC. I've only heard about this type of activity through rumors until I witnessed the actual event last night. It was unreal to see everything unfolding in front of me.

The reverend was highly skilled in what he did. He used his power and the trust that his patient had in him. Dying patients are vulnerable, and he knew that well. Those who are utterly alone without family members by their side are even more helpless.

It was around 2 a.m., and Reverend John was called in at my patient, Mr. Small's, request. Mr. Small was dying from cancer.

Getting the Reverend was easy because he was on call. "No worries, we are available 24/7." Reverend John is in his early 60s, mild-mannered, with glasses and oily blond hair combed toward the back.

The Reverend opened his leather Bible, then stood right next to Mr. Small. Mr. Small was in his 80s. You could see the severity of his suffering through his skin-and-bone features. His cancer-withered sunken eyes were partly closed as if he was too exhausted to close them all the way, but he did manage to hold his rosary in his right hand.

Reverend John gently put his right hand over Mr. Small's emaciated hands. The Reverend's well-groomed physical appearance was utterly opposite of Mr. Small's overgrown and unkempt gray hair that rested on his pillow. Mr. Small slowly opened his mouth, gasping to breathe. He was gasping for air, even with an oxygen mask.

Mr. Small said, "Pastor...Help... me out, so I...I...can go... to...heaven. I...need...a...re...demp...tion."

Reverend John looked down upon the old man's half-closed, cataract-covered blue eyes. There was a pause and moment of stillness, where Reverend John's soft and warm gaze met with Mr. Small's weak and fearful eyes. Reverend John then began reciting the phrase:

"Come to me all you who are weary and burdened, and I will give you rest. For God so loved the world that he gave his one and only Son, that whoever believes in him shall not perish but have eternal life."

With that, the patient replied with all the energy left in him, "Oh, Pastor, Th…ank…you. I, I…want to donate everything…I have…to…this hospital."

Right after Mr. Small completed the sentence, a man in his late 30s with short stature, circular glasses, and an exquisite lawyerly appearance briskly pulled a paper out of his black leather briefcase. He then quickly brought the document closer to the dying man's face and started to recite.

"I, Warren J. Small, leave the entirety of my estate, in excess of 10 million dollars, to the Angels Medical Center non-profit organization."

The lawyer then said in a polite, firm, yet businesslike tone of voice, "Mr. Small, please sign here if this is your wish." After the lawyer collected Mr. Small's signature, he signed his own name to make the "gift" official. As soon as the signature process was complete, the lawyer stepped back, allowing Reverend John to proceed with the next step.

As Reverend John had clearly done many times before, he began to pray for Mr. Small in his calm and soothing voice:

> *O Lord, lift up my soul,*
> *You embraced me with Your tender love,*
> *welcome me into Your paradise,*
> *where there will be no sorrow, no weeping or pain,*
> *but the peace and joy, and eternal rest*
> *with your Son and the Holy Spirit*
> *-Amen.*

Mr. Small moaned with pain. He began moving his left hand, appearing to be palpating and searching for something on his chest, but he moved slowly as if he was holding onto something heavy, using all the energy left within him. A few seconds later, he finally grabbed onto the Morphine PCA button in his left hand, shaking. He let out a big sigh of relief, but it came out as a whimper, as he pushed the PCA button with his left thumb. Seconds later, Mr. Small stopped his gasping breaths altogether, then there was complete silence, his dark and sunken eyes still gazing in mid-air. For a while, no one moved.

Ginger put down the pen, reread what she'd written, and felt the heaviness of it all come crashing down on her. She didn't want to work at that hospital anymore.

She thought of her brother's last letter that she'd received just a few days earlier. He had urged her to get a life, focus on something other than work. There'd also been a subtle nudging, a reminder that her parents were eager for her to settle down and get married. It had been a while since she'd dated, but she agreed that focusing on something other than work would be good for her.

Deep down, though, she didn't think it would solve her problems. She recognized the feeling she was experiencing. It was the same feeling she had when she knew she had to leave Saudi Arabia. It felt a bit like she was drowning.

CHAPTER 10

Seattle, Washington
March 20, 2020

A decision had been made that in order to provide consistency of care, and to fix a shortage of nursing staffing, two sets of nurses would work on Ginger round-the-clock, seven days a week, until Ginger showed some improvement and they could hire some more nurses. That meant that Hyun was now required to work mandatory overtime on top of her usual three twelve-hour shifts with Clara, while Joe and Matthew handled the night shift. For Hyun, getting used to the overtime had been grueling now that she was without even one day's break.

As the night shift came, she gave her report to Dr. Brown.

"The second hemodialysis was completed this afternoon. BUN and GFR are still way off," Hyun reported.

"Since it's right after the dialysis, let's wait and keep monitoring the level. Hopefully, it improves by tomorrow. I see she put out some urine," Dr. Brown said, pointing at Ginger's Foley bag. "The color is slightly lighter. That's a good sign."

"Her trop also is lower than yesterday. It's 4," Dr. Lim chimed in. "It's encouraging."

Dr. Lee spoke up. "All we can do is pray. Time will tell."

The doctors and Clara finally left the room. Hyun could hear Clara outside, talking and flirting with Tom the RT. It sounded like they were heading out for a smoke together, even though their shift would be over in less than thirty minutes.

Hyun bit her lip. She could also hear Joe in the hall, talking to one of the doctors about Ginger. He was a Caucasian nurse like Clara, but had a completely opposite work ethic. He carried himself professionally, was never late for work, didn't dump his work on others, and was respectful towards his coworkers, including Hyun. She trusted her patient with him.

"You're going to have a good night, aren't you?" Hyun asked Ginger softly.

She turned on the television in the room, hoping it would stimulate Ginger's brain. The news, unfortunately, was just as depressing as it had been since everything had started. The announcers droned on about the number of deaths nationally and worldwide.

Then something that caught her attention. It was a slogan—a rallying cry being picked up by healthcare workers across the nation. It made sense. Hyun thought of her own husband at home, his business shuttered because of the virus.

She bent down close and whispered to Ginger. "You need to wake up and shout these slogans with us. We need to stick together."

There was another clip of nurses holding up the sign. Hyun nodded in solidarity.

"You hear that, Ginger?" Hyun asked. "It's a new campaign. From front-line workers, like us. 'We stayed at work for you, stay at home for us.'"

Ginger didn't respond, and Hyun hadn't expected her to. Some of the other nurses didn't get why Hyun talked to patients who were unconscious. But in Hyun's mind, until science could prove without a doubt that the unconscious couldn't hear anything, then she planned to go on talking to them. She believed it was therapeutic for both the patients and their care providers—especially as lately, hers was the only friendly voice her patients would hear, primarily because their loved ones were no longer being let into hospitals.

But it hurt Hyun, because she knew there were patients who were dying alone who had families desperate to visit them. Even sadder to her were those patients who didn't have anyone who wanted to see them. Regardless of their circumstances, Hyun believed that at least nurses could be voices in their patients' ears, reminding them that life was worth living and that there was hope, no matter how hard the struggle.

"Come on, Ginger," she whispered encouragingly. "Say it with me. 'We stayed at work for you, stay at home for us.'"

Kirkland, Washington
July 2004

"Stay at home?" Ginger repeated, staring disbelievingly at the man sitting across the table from her. Ronald was thin and brown-haired, with blue eyes that were staring earnestly at her.

He was an engineer who worked with her brother, Daehan, at Boeing. That's why she had agreed to go on this blind date with him while visiting her brother and checking out the area hospitals. Daehan and his wife, Mary, had recently moved to Kirkland, Washington, trying to get away from the hustle and bustle of downtown Seattle.

"Of course. I understand your culture, and I want to respect it," he said, trying to sound sincere. "I've always found the Asian cultures to be so much more…refined than our western cultures. That's why I'm interested in traditional Asian women. I want you to stay home and take care of the family."

He smiled at her, clearly trying to be charming. But she saw right through him.

"You think I don't want to work?" she asked.

"Not at all. I know how hard a worker you are. Daehan talks about you all the time. I just know you'd be happier in a more natural role."

He reached across the table and took her hand. She pulled it away quickly, much to his surprise.

"I'm sorry, but what you're describing…I'm not interested," she said.

She stood abruptly and left the coffee house. Outside, she walked a couple of blocks before hailing a taxi to take her back to Daehan and Mary's house.

When she arrived, Mary was in the kitchen preparing dinner.

"That was fast," Mary commented as Ginger sat down with a disgusted sigh on one of the stools at the kitchen counter.

"Have you met that guy?" Ginger asked.

"Ronald? Once, at a Christmas party," Mary said, forehead wrinkling in concentration. "Why?"

"I can't believe Daehan would set me up with him. He's looking for a 'traditional Asian wife,'" she said, making air quotes with her fingers.

Mary shook her head, incredulous.

"He said he would expect me to quit my job and stay home."

"What, are we living in the thirties?" Mary exclaimed.

"Right? How could Daehan do that to me?"

"I'm sure he didn't know," Mary said, quick to defend her husband.

Ginger stared for a moment at her sister-in-law. She hadn't been able to spend much time with her brother and his wife, and suddenly, Ginger wondered if her brother's belief towards women were the same as Ronald's. Ginger felt an urgent need to find out.

"Daehan doesn't treat you that way, does he?" she asked Mary cautiously.

Mary laughed heartily. "Never! He's not that type at all."

Ginger felt relieved. "I know he isn't that type of person, but I just had to ask. Where is he anyway?"

"At the store. I was missing some ingredients for dinner. He's bringing home KFC after that."

"I thought you were making dinner?" Ginger asked, confused.

"This is for tomorrow night. It needs time to marinate."

"Is there something special going on tomorrow night?"

"Yes, he's asked a coworker over for dinner." Mary looked at her sheepishly. "To meet you."

Ginger waved her hands in the air, as if to fend off that idea. She heard the garage door open and close.

"Oh no, not another blind date." Ginger groaned.

Moments later, Daehan appeared, carrying a bucket of chicken and some grocery bags.

"What's wrong with blind dates?" her brother asked as he set everything down on the counter.

"Everything, especially when the men have unrealistic expectations," Ginger said.

"What expectations?" Daehan asked with a frown.

"Ronald wants a female slave," Mary said pertly. "One who never leaves the house."

"What? You're kidding me," Daehan said, looking genuinely surprised.

"Brother, I wish I was."

"I'm sorry, sis. I had no idea."

"I created an account a couple of days ago on a dating website. I'll give it a try, but I'm done with blind dates."

Daehan shook his head. "At least have dinner with us tomorrow night and meet David. He's been going on and on about you ever since he saw your picture on my desk at work six months ago. He mentioned you're beautiful."

"She *is* beautiful," Mary echoed.

"I'm also smart. Did you tell him that?" Ginger asked, feeling dubious.

"Repeatedly. He likes smart women."

"Is he Asian?" Ginger asked.

"No, Caucasian. Not all Caucasians are like Ronald, sis."

"Brother, I'm just afraid he is…"

"I don't see how he could be. His cousin married a Japanese woman who is a pharmacist. He always says they are the perfect couple."

"She wasn't expected to quit her job?" Ginger asked.

"No, she still works."

Ginger nodded her head slowly. "Okay, I'll have dinner with you tomorrow night and meet him. But no promises."

Daehan smiled at her. "I just hope you like him. He's a really funny guy. Mom and Dad met him when they were out here visiting last."

"I wish we could convince them to move here," Ginger said with a twinge of sadness.

"I know. I had a long conversation with them last week, trying again to get through to them."

"Let me guess. They said that at eighty, they don't want to uproot their lives. All their friends are in Korea, and they've put too much time into their garden," Ginger said, remembering her past conversations with her parents.

"Yes, and they don't know English and think it will just be too much to have to adjust to a new culture, particularly when they don't understand the language. They like visiting, and think it's beautiful here and in Alaska, but they don't want to be a burden to either of us."

"They wouldn't be a burden," Ginger protested.

"I know, sis, but they don't see it that way. When I think of all they did to help me, my friends…" he drifted off as he struggled with emotion. Ginger knew Daehan was remembering the days when their parents had housed and fed half the militia.

She put a hand on his arm. "They don't want our help," she said softly. "And, for now at least, it seems like they don't need it. Maybe one day that will change, but until then…"

"I know, we have to respect their wishes," he said with a sigh.

"It's just hard. I worry about them because of their age. The video calls just aren't enough."

After partaking in the fried chicken, Ginger retreated to the guest room. She logged onto her online dating profile and scrolled through various options. She finally accepted two contact requests, one from a Korean man and the other from a Filipino one. They had both been born and raised in America. She just hoped they both had more realistic expectations of what they wanted in a girlfriend, let alone a wife.

It was late when she finally turned in, and she struggled to fall asleep. It felt like the world was closing in on her, that everything was restricting her. She knew her brother and her parents just wanted what was best for her. However, they weren't the ones who would have to live with whomever she chose. She needed a guy who would treat her as an equal, who wouldn't try to suffocate or stifle her.

She tossed and turned. She finally kicked free of the covers, sending them crashing to the floor. With her legs unfettered, she finally fell asleep.

CHAPTER 11

Seattle, Washington
March 22, 2020

"Oh man, there isn't much progress on her condition…" Dr. Khan muttered, pacing anxiously near Ginger's bed. Dr. Lim, the cardiologist, stood to Ginger's left and carefully reviewed the 12-lead EKG results, which had just been generated by the tech. "I see mild ST depression on her rhythm, but that's expected since her cardiac enzyme was over six when she first arrived at Pine Health. The rates are similar to yesterday. Her heart is holding on, at least."

"Her creatinine level is creeping up again though, and the numbers in BUN are not that great either," Dr. Khan pointed out.

Dr. Brown replied, "I can order another round of dialysis and an ultrasound of the kidneys. I'll go ahead and type in the orders now."

"You got it," Hyun replied. She began preparing for another dialysis on the ECMO, combining it with the CRRT machine.

The doctors left the room, and Hyun kept working while Clara reviewed IV medications. One of the IV pumps had been beeping nonstop since the shift change that morning. Hyun was growing concerned because the beeping meant there was a delay in medication administration to Ginger. However, Clara never asked Hyun for advice. Instead, she went out and got one of the new graduates to troubleshoot the problematic IV pump, yet the beeping continued.

Finally, Hyun approached Clara. "Can I help you?"

Flustered, Clara lifted her head up from the IV pump, "I guess…hmmm…Let me pick your brain. Can you take a look at this dumb pump and see why this sucker is giving me such a problem? But only do it if you know how!"

Hyun did not like Clara's arrogant and condescending attitude but, as always, she had to put her personal frustration aside. Patient care was the first priority.

She quickly assessed Ginger's central line, IV line connection, the pump, and how the medications were hung at the pole. Immediately, she saw the problem. It was the same problem Hyun had gone over with Clara before. In fact, this was the fourth time that Hyun was going to have to explain the same issue to her.

"Clara, we have to flush the central line on this port first. If the line flushes well with good blood return, then we should re-wire this TPN and lipid. Since the lipid must infuse extremely slowly at 12cc/hr., you should connect it directly to the patient, then add TPN line over the lipid," Hyun paused, trying to think of the best way to get through to Clara. "Think of it like this: the TPN line works as a gentle push from behind when you are sledding on snow. The TPN pushes lipid at 65cc/hr. It is easy if you think of the lipid as snow since it is pale white."

Sure enough, after Hyun corrected the problem, the TPN and lipid infused seamlessly. But she worried about how Clara, as a nurse, wasn't able to perform such a straightforward task, much less troubleshoot the problem even after the third time she'd been educated on the issue. She still wired the line the opposite way, which led the lipid line to stall and beep.

Clara shrugged at Hyun's correction and began to assess the SCD compression sleeves on Ginger's legs, not offering so much as a simple "thank you" to Hyun.

"Her legs seem swollen," Clara said after a moment. "Can you help me assess them?" Assessing the patient's legs was a two-person job, especially if the patient was unconscious, and hooked up to additional devices such as an ECMO line that was placed on either side of the groin.

Hyun looked at Ginger's desperately swollen legs. Just looking at the tight-stretched skin made her own legs ache in sympathy. She knew if Ginger were awake, she would be in incredible pain. The sight was especially concerning because the swelling hadn't been there yesterday.

She must have a circulatory problem...or worse.

"Look at this," Hyun said.

"I see it," Clara answered.

The white SCD sleeves were stained with a yellowish color because some of the fluids squeezed out of Ginger's skin when the SCD machine applied pressure intermittently to promote the circulation of the legs.

Hyun lifted up Ginger's left leg. Clara wrapped it with kerlix gauze, then switched to a large-sized SCD by unsnapping from the tube and removing the small, stained SCD.

As Hyun was holding Ginger's leg, she realized with a start how cold it was to the touch. Fear knifed through her. She looked closer and saw a tiny black spot on Ginger's left big toe.

"Clara, I think there's something else going on with Ginger's body besides the complication we're already aware of. Take a look at the gangrene-looking toe here and feel how cold the legs are. There are no signs of blood returning to her toenails at all."

After Hyun put down Ginger's legs, she assessed Ginger's arms. "Fortunately, her arms and hands are warm and have a good capillary refill. I think we should hold off from reapplying SCD and notify Dr. Khan ASAP."

"Damn! Things don't look good," Clara exclaimed. "I'll page Dr. Khan now."

Hyun carefully examined Ginger's other leg and foot while Dr. Khan finally responded to Clara's page.

"Dr. Khan said she'd be assessing Ginger's legs and the big toe as soon as she is done taking care of emergencies with other COVID patients."

"I hope she hurries. If she doesn't arrive in the next five minutes, I'm activating RRT," Hyun said, referring to a rapid response team. She was now very worried that Ginger was about to become another COVID-related emergency.

Hyun and Clara continued to work on Ginger. For Hyun, the five minutes that passed felt more like five hours. Just when she was about to press the yellow RRT button on the wall, Ginger suddenly twitched.

Hyun and Clara both paused at the threshold of the room and stared for a moment.

Suddenly, Ginger's body began seizing and bucking. She was fighting against the ventilator.

Hyun quickly pushed the "code blue" button on the wall. Ginger's heart rhythm changed to SVT—an abnormally fast heart rate—in the 180s.

The entire care team arrived minutes after hearing the code blue overhead announcement. Everyone moved under Dr. Khan's lead.

"Give 1mg of IV Ativan now, then administer Dilantin IV. Let's run a basic blood test, stat EKG, head CT, EEG, ultrasound of her legs, arms, and the heart ECHO. I'll type in all these orders in a few minutes," Dr. Khan ordered.

"Got it," Hyun stated clearly.

"Wonder what's going on…" Dr. Lim said worriedly while she listened to Ginger's heart tone with her stethoscope, carefully assessing Ginger and the cardiac monitor.

"Let's treat her symptoms now and investigate the reason for the sudden dive of her condition later." Dr. Khan declared.

Hyun took over administering the stat medications to Ginger, working quickly. At last, Ginger stopped seizing and her condition stabilized.

"Let's get an ultrasound on those legs and arms, stat!" Dr. Khan ordered.

"Don't you give up on us," Hyun whispered to Ginger.

As soon as the results of the ultrasound came back, the doctors all looked them over. From their grim expressions, Hyun knew it wasn't good news.

"We need to call her family," Dr. Khan said.

"Why, what is it?" Clara asked.

"Her legs are filled with blood clots."

"Oh no!" Hyun exclaimed.

Dr. Khan nodded grimly. "We still have a chance to save the patient, but her legs aren't salvageable."

Kirkland, Washington
July 2004

"**M**y friendship with Ronald is unsalvageable," Ginger overheard Daehan say the next morning.

"Are you sure?" Mary asked.

"How can it not be? What can he possibly think of me if he thinks he can treat my sister that way?"

"It has nothing to do with you. You know how people make assumptions. The stereotype is out there, and not without reason."

"I know, but he should have known better. It's my fault. I should have been clear with him."

"Ginger is a grown woman. She doesn't need you to fight her battles for her," Mary said gently.

Ginger stood just out of sight, nodding her head in agreement as she listened to the couple. She wasn't comfortable eavesdropping, but she didn't know how to interrupt the conversation without making things even more awkward.

"Tonight will be different. David's a good guy," Daehan said doggedly.

Ginger turned and headed back to her room. She felt terrible that Daehan might have lost Ronald as a friend, but she knew that was simply who her brother was. He would never stand for Ronald's unreasonable expectations and twisted desires towards women.

She decided the least she could do was give David a fair shot, especially since Daehan seemed to hold him in high regard.

When dinner came, it was interesting. True to his reputation, David was funny. He also kept smiling at Ginger in a way that made her blush more than once.

"I have to say that you're even more beautiful than your picture," he told her quietly during a lull in the conversation.

"Thank you," she said.

"Daehan tells me you're a nurse."

"I am."

"He also tells me that you're currently working in Alaska. I'm hoping he can convince you to move down here. We have a shortage of good nurses…and beautiful women."

Even though he was complimenting her, there was something about his tone that made her uncomfortable. Maybe it was that he was so direct, it felt almost pushy. Then again, at least she knew where she stood. She'd been on dates before where she couldn't tell what the guy thought about her at all.

David stayed well after dessert and dropped several more hints about how much better Seattle and Kirkland would be for her, for *them*. It was presumptuous of him, but clearly, he seemed to think that because she was only visiting for a few days, he had to make his feelings known to her.

When it was finally time for him to leave, he asked if she would walk him to his car. Daehan nodded at her encouragingly. She wondered what David might say to her in private without her brother and sister-in-law listening. She wasn't sure if he would make his feelings even clearer or if he was the kind of guy who was only talkative in a crowd.

But it was a short walk to the car, so she stood and nodded at him.

"It was a pleasure meeting you," she said once they reached his car.

There had been nothing wrong with the dinner, but she hadn't felt any kind of attraction to him, which she knew would disappoint her brother. Still, she was willing to keep an open mind. People could be nervous on blind dates, particularly when family members were present.

David turned to her with a smile. Without warning, he put his hand behind her head and tried to pull her toward him. Startled, she resisted.

"Come here," he insisted.

"What are you doing?" she asked.

"Getting a goodnight kiss. The first of many."

She put a hand on his chest and pushed him away.

He frowned. "What's with you?"

"I choose who I give a kiss to," she said, anger flooding her.

"I want to be with you. Maybe I wasn't clear. I'm choosing you," David said, his voice arrogant.

"Well, I'm not choosing you," she said.

He had the nerve to look genuinely shocked. "I don't understand. What's wrong with you?"

"Wrong with me? Nothing. I'm normal. Your expectations are the problem. Not all Asian women are submissive. And we have opinions of our own."

"That's not what I've heard."

"Well, then hear this. Go away. I'm not interested in you. I'm not a flower you can bend to your will. And, by the way, well-balanced, confident men don't look for a submissive woman."

He stood there with a dumbfounded expression on his face. She turned, went back into the house, and slammed the door behind her.

Ginger stormed into the kitchen and Daehan looked up at her. He was up to his elbows in dirty dishes in the sink. His hopeful expression quickly changed to one of concern.

"What's wrong, sis?"

She shook her head. "Please don't set me up with any more of your friends."

"What did he do?"

"He tried to force me to kiss him."

Daehan let go of the dishes, brow furrowing in anger, soap bubbles clinging to his hands as they curled into fists. He headed for the front door.

"Forget it," she said to him, shaking her head. "He's probably gone by now. Besides, I don't want you to make things difficult for yourself at work."

"The only one who's going to find work difficult is him," Daehan growled, turning to look at her.

She smiled at his protectiveness, then impulsively hugged him. He returned the embrace, getting the back of her shirt wet and soapy. She didn't mind at all.

"Thank you for being a good brother and looking out for me."

CHAPTER 12

Seattle, Washington
March 22, 2020

"You're a good brother," Hyun told Daehan over the video call.

Daehan's face was pale and grief-stricken.

"How did we get here?" he asked shakily, clearly still reeling from the news. "How did I let this happen?"

"It's not your fault," Hyun said firmly. "It's no one's fault,"

It really wasn't her place to say so, but over the last several days, she was the one who'd had the most contact with Ginger's family.

Behind her, Dr. Khan and Dr. Porter both nodded in agreement.

"Is there no other way?" Daehan asked, his voice pleading.

Dr. Porter cleared his throat. "Your sister developed severe blood clots in both legs. We must amputate them below the knees as soon as possible. If we don't, she will almost certainly die."

"You're asking me to take away her legs. How can I make that decision? How is she going to feel? What is she going to say when she wakes up and realizes they're gone?"

"If you don't do this, she'll never wake up," Dr. Khan asserted.

Daehan's face crumpled in despair. "How do I know that? And how do I know the surgery or complications from it won't kill her?"

"There is always a risk," Dr. Porter said evenly.

"Is that what you told Talia Goldenberg's parents?" Daehan asked pointedly.

Hyun struggled to keep her face neutral. He was referencing a young woman who had tragically died in their hospital after having spinal surgery several years ago. Many had since questioned whether or not that surgery had been done correctly.

"Look, Mr. Kim, every minute you wait to decide, your sister's survival rate decreases. We need your decision now," Dr. Porter said firmly.

Daehan hesitated, closing his eyes. Hyun's heart broke for him. His wife, Mary, reached out and grasped his hands.

After a moment, he let out a heart-wrenching sigh and tears began to roll down his cheeks. "Go ahead and do it," he said, giving his verbal consent.

Anchorage, Alaska
August 2004

"What are you waiting for? Just decide already," Ginger told herself.

She hit the button, officially canceling her online dating subscription. Since returning to Alaska three days earlier, she'd had two disastrous dates. Even though both men had been born and raised in America, and believed that a woman should work outside the home...they also believed she should have all the "traditional" responsibilities at home. Meaning double the burden for her.

One of them had actually told her that his parents raised him to be a man who should never set foot in the kitchen or otherwise be caught doing "women's work." Both guys also admitted that they'd lied in their online profiles. They didn't want a strong, independent woman. They wanted a submissive wife who would obey them, do all the household work, and hand over her earnings to them.

"What is wrong with men?" she asked herself out loud, exasperated.

She sighed, realizing it couldn't possibly be all men—just the ones she was finding. She had to give up on dating for the moment. Her parents wouldn't be happy, but she couldn't keep making herself crazy over this.

Not going on dates also freed her up to do other things. She picked up a flyer for the Smile Autism Center. The center was looking for volunteers, and something inside tugged at her. She couldn't help but feel there was more that she had to offer the world, so maybe the SAC was where she'd figure it out.

It was Ginger's second day volunteering at the center. She was on a break, and she sat at a table in the breakroom, eating her lunch as she read through some pamphlets on autism. She knew what autism was, but hadn't had much exposure to people who had it, so she wanted to educate herself as best as she could to be more helpful as a volunteer.

A tired-looking woman with brown hair and blue eyes walked up to her. "Is this seat taken?" she asked, indicating the other chair at Ginger's table.

"No, feel free," Ginger said, gesturing for the woman to take a seat.

"Thank you."

The woman pulled out the chair and collapsed into it with a weary sigh. She had hot chocolate in her hand and placed an apple in front of her. She sat staring at both for a moment, then she looked up at Ginger.

"You're new here, aren't you?"

"Yes, I'm Ginger," Ginger said, looking up from her reading.

"Autumn. It's nice to meet you," the woman said, offering her hand.

Ginger shook it and, assuming that was the end of their interaction, went back to reading.

"Studying up on autism?" Autumn asked.

"Yes," Ginger said, somewhat surprised the woman was still talking to her.

"Ask me anything. I know it all." The woman sighed again. "At least, I think I do until I realize that no one knows anything."

"Are you okay?" Ginger asked, sensing Autumn's strain.

"I'm sorry. I'm just having a tough day. My twin boys, Noah and Liam, are autistic."

"How old are they?" Ginger asked.

"They're five, and they're both non-verbal."

"That must be hard. Why is today so bad in particular?"

Autumn shook her head. "You know, discrimination against those with disabilities continues to blow my mind. Just when I think it can't get any worse, it does. I have to fight the government to get equal education opportunities. I'm fighting to get an expansion of medical coverage. I'm fighting to get funding for those in the community who need it. Basically, I'm just fighting all the time, and I'm tired."

"I understand," Ginger said slowly.

Autumn looked at her contemplatively. "Something tells me you do. You know, I thought I'd seen the worst type of discrimination when I worked in Saudi Arabia, but what I see here is just...evil."

"I worked in Saudi Arabia!" Ginger said in surprise.

"Really?" Autumn wondered, eyes widening. "I worked at King Faisal Hospital."

"So did I!" Ginger said excitedly. "I worked there from 1998 to 2002."

"I was there in 1998," Autumn said. "Were you in the dorm?"

"Yes! It's too bad we never ran into each other."

"It was a big place."

To Ginger's delight, her conversation with Autumn seemed to flow naturally. Though they hadn't run into each other while working at King Faisal, they shared similar experiences. They even knew a few people in common.

By the end of the break, they exchanged numbers, and Ginger found herself volunteering to babysit Autumn's twins. She even found herself considering making a change in her own life. Autumn was a psych nurse who worked at a different hospital. The more Ginger thought about it, the more she thought that perhaps life would be more rewarding for her if she made a move.

When Ginger got home, she found she had received a letter from Eungi with more pictures of her and her family. After having dinner, Ginger eagerly sat down to write to Eungi about her new friend.

CHAPTER 13

Seattle, Washington
March 23, 2020

Hyun found herself praying that Ginger would finally turn a corner and start to recover. It was the day after Ginger's legs had been amputated, and it was an adjustment even for Hyun, who had to remind herself that there were no longer lower legs and feet for her to check over.

Ginger had survived the bilateral below-knee amputation. As with any surgery, infection was a real concern. Given the state of her health, Hyun knew Ginger couldn't sustain another trauma, so she was watching everything—including Clara—with more paranoia than usual.

While Hyun worked, Clara made the video call to Daehan and Mary to report on Ginger's condition. Hyun felt her own throat constrict as she heard the couple start to cry once they saw Ginger's stumps wrapped in white surgical gauze.

"We're sorry," Daehan said, as if he had anything to apologize for. "We just feel so bad for Ginger."

We all do, Hyun thought.

Anchorage, Alaska
August 2009

"No peeking," Autumn said.

Ginger kept her eyes tightly shut, even though the curiosity was killing her. She could feel Autumn's boys, Liam and Noah, sitting on either side of her, wiggling with excitement.

They were sitting at a picnic bench, staring out at the water. Ginger and Autumn had taken the boys on their first fishing trip. The actual fishing had only lasted a couple of minutes before it lost the twins' attention, but Ginger was just happy to be out in nature, hanging out with her friend.

"What is going on?" Ginger asked, putting an arm around each boy.

The last five years since Ginger had first met Autumn had been wonderful. When she'd first met Autumn, her story had excited sympathy, almost pity, from Ginger. Now, Autumn was her closest friend, aside from Eungi, and her boys were as dear to Ginger as if they were her nephews. She respected and admired Autumn a great deal and was happy to help her whenever she could.

"Well, we met five years ago today," Autumn said. "And the boys and I wanted you to know how much you've changed our lives. You've helped us so much. You could say you're our hero. Hold out your hands."

Ginger did so, and felt something being placed into her hands. It felt light, and the texture was unfamiliar.

"Open your eyes," Autumn said.

Ginger did, and gaped at what she was holding. It was a small, homemade wooden trophy topped with a nurse standing in a superhero-like pose, with her hands on her hips, painted in gold.

Ginger's face beamed as she read the inscription.

Ginger Kim — Nurse, Friend, Hero who champions the underdog.

Both boys clapped their hands, copying their mother.

"I love it. Thank you," Ginger told them tenderly as she hugged all three of them.

Autumn motioned to the twins to give Ginger a kiss on the cheek, and they each did. However, Autumn noticed Ginger was more quiet than usual, and she stared at Ginger in confusion.

"Okay, boys, time for a nap," Autumn said, trying to keep her voice neutral. She had set up a tent with some sleeping bags so the boys wouldn't miss their afternoon slumber.

Ginger sat on the bench, struggling to get a hold of herself while Autumn got the boys settled down. Each of them wore a noise-canceling headset so that sudden or loud sounds wouldn't disturb them. It was an unfortunate necessity of taking them out anywhere, even in nature.

When Autumn finally came back, she grabbed two water bottles out of the cooler and handed one to Ginger before sitting down next to her.

"What's wrong? Is there something bothering you?" Autumn asked softly.

Ginger's heart was filled with misery. She didn't want to bring her friend down, but she needed to get something off her chest. She'd been writing letters to Eungi, but some days it felt more like she was writing in a journal than actually talking things through. Of course, Eungi responded when she could, but she had her own life and her hands were often full with her family. Besides, she couldn't truly understand some of the experiences Ginger was going through since Eungi had never worked in the U.S. So while Eungi was sympathetic, she didn't really get it most of the time.

"I love my trophy," Ginger said, looking down at it. She was still clutching it in her hands.

"I'm glad you like it. It's kind of childish, but I had fun carving it, and the boys also seemed to enjoy painting it," Autumn said cheerfully.

Ginger gave her a weak smile. She felt bad. She just didn't feel like she deserved the trophy. She never discussed all the darkness and ugliness she was experiencing at AMC with Autumn. Autumn had to deal with so much in her life that Ginger didn't want to burden her with her own problems.

However, Ginger knew that one could hold a burden only for so long. She wanted to talk to Autumn about everything that was happening in AMC, but only when the time was right. After all, if anyone understood what discrimination and isolation felt like, it was Autumn. No additional explanation would be required.

"I feel like I fail people," Ginger finally said in a barely audible voice, trying to force the words out around the lump in her throat.

"Fail people? Oh, honey, you never fail anyone. You're the best nurse I know, and no one could ask for a more selfless, caring friend," Autumn said soothingly. "I don't know how I would have survived these last five years without your help. I don't know how I would have managed without you listening to all my woes dealing with bureaucratic red tape."

Autumn rubbed Ginger's shoulder as Ginger just put her head down and let out the sobs that she'd been trying to hold in. They sat there for several minutes, Autumn rubbing her shoulders while Ginger's grief overwhelmed her.

"Some days, I feel so helpless and worse than useless," Ginger confessed, her voice still cracking.

"I don't understand," Autumn said, her own voice trembling with emotion. "Who is it you think you've failed?"

Ginger shook her head, not wanting to say.

"Please, tell me what's going on. I'm dying here!" Autumn begged.

Ginger forced herself to take several deep breaths, and took a sip of water. It helped clear her head somewhat, and she was finally able to look at Autumn.

"The hospital is so corrupt. And the bullying and the discrimination are unbearable. I've been putting up with so much for such a long time. Now I'm up to my neck."

Autumn blinked at her slowly, then frowned. "What do you mean?" she asked.

It all came pouring out of Ginger, everything she'd held back. She told Autumn what had happened to Maria and the rampant racism she and others still had to endure during every single shift. She even told her about the premature discharge of countless patients, as well as the on-going deathbed vigils where the hospital all but forced patients to sign away their fortunes.

Throughout it all, Autumn listened carefully, nodding from time to time. Ginger could tell by the look on her face that some of her story was no surprise to her.

When Ginger had finally said all she could, Autumn gave her a quick hug. "There are assholes everywhere," Autumn said with a sigh. "I'm sorry you've had a rough time of it. I feel awful you've felt that you've had to keep all of this to yourself for so long. I can only imagine how difficult it's been for you to try to deal with that environment all by yourself."

"I feel like I could have done more for Maria, or for myself for that matter. I just feel so powerless. I'm all alone in this. Everyone else just puts their head down and keeps on going as if nothing is bothering them."

"I think you did your best to support Maria. Unfortunately, racism is a problem everywhere, not just at your hospital."

"Someone has to take a stand, change things," Ginger muttered.

"As a white nurse, I've helped some Black and Asian nurses try it before," Autumn said. "We've taken our discrimination complaints all the way to the board. A couple of nurses even tried to sue. I've never seen anything ever come of it though. It was just a lot of misery and heartbreak for them with no change."

"How can that be?"

"Because the people in charge are masters at manipulating the law. The hospitals have teams of lawyers who know labor laws inside and out. They know how to play the EEOC, and they turn investigations into a joke."

Ginger hunched her shoulders, feeling worse. Autumn, seeming to sense that, once again put her hand on Ginger's shoulder.

"I don't mean that you should give up. More than anyone, I understand how hard this is and how the injustices eat away at you. You know the fight I've been going through trying to get care and education for my boys." Autumn shook her head in frustration. "Autism research isn't well-funded. Health insurance coverage for autism-related illness is minimal. What's worse, no one wants to get involved. I'm not rich, so I can't afford all the private tutoring and education for my kids that they need. I can't pay all their medical expenses out of my own pocket. And the longer this goes on, the more I resent the government, the insurance companies, everyone."

"But you don't give up," Ginger said, drying her tears.

"That's because I'd rather die for the cause than die without having done anything. I mean, isn't that why we got into medicine in the first place? To help and make a difference in our healthcare?"

Ginger thought of the old promise she had made to God while huddled in her family's living room during the Gwangju massacre. It may have been that childhood promise that set her on the path to nursing, but helping people and making a difference in human life was the foundation of who she was. Wanting to keep that contract with herself had never changed for her.

"Yes, it is," Ginger said, feeling a lump in her throat. "But I don't think I can just stand and watch the hospital take patients' property on their deathbeds or prematurely discharge sick patients when it's obvious that they will come right back in ED."

Autumn's face looked gloomy and pained. "I hate to say this, but I don't think it's a fight you can win."

"You don't think so?" Ginger replied, unconvinced as she gazed at the horizon.

"When it comes to the deathbed pressure to donate to the hospital, it will be your word against the hospital's. I mean, it's going to be impossible to prove, unless other nurses step forward. But who's going to risk their job? The patients are dead, and they can't testify about what kind of pressure they did or did not feel."

Ginger sat silently, listening.

"Patients who are being prematurely discharged won't stand with you. In many cases, because of their illness, they don't have the mental or physical capacity to be involved in a lawsuit. They probably don't have money to hire lawyers either. Plus, they don't want any kind of retaliation when it comes to continued treatment. Face it. The hospital has millions of dollars and lawyers just sitting around ready to jump on these kinds of things. And, of course, the second you make noise about a lawsuit, they'll come after you. They'll come up with some terrible made-up stories to discredit you. They'll probably even try to make it so you can't work as a nurse again."

While Ginger listened to her friend's lecture, she remembered the retribution against her brother Daehan, along with the many others who had fought against General Jun in South Korea. The consequences were overwhelmingly painful, and people still had to live with them today.

However, deep down, she felt if Daehan were in her position, he would do more to stop what was going on in the hospital.

Autumn continued, "You know, some people move to the U.S. simply believing in the American dream. But achieving this dream requires a lot of sacrifices, especially when it's jerks who run the show. If you try to fight this battle, you could lose everything."

In her heart, Ginger knew Autumn was telling the truth. It was just so maddening to feel so helpless. It almost felt as though she was right back in her parents' living room, helplessly huddled in the dark and hiding, while everyone else was off fighting and risking their lives.

Ginger knew there must be some way to fight for her belief. She understood Autumn wanted to protect her from being fired or possible legal battles. At the same time, Autumn clearly would not give up the fight for her children. Ginger did not want to give up her fight either...but how?

That's something I have to figure out.

Ginger let out a long sigh.

"You know, maybe we both need a change," Autumn said solemnly.

"What do you mean?" Ginger asked, puzzled.

"I can't do anything more here. I've hit the final roadblock. My boys need more than I can get for them here, so I've been looking at UW in Washington state. They have a good treatment team and a research program on autism. I've run out of time to sit here and wait for things to change. If we move to Washington, the boys will have access to more education and therapy options."

Suddenly, it felt like a weight had been lifted off Ginger's chest. She took a deep breath. For a while, she had been thinking about moving closer to Daehan and Mary. They had been pushing for it. But she hadn't wanted to leave Autumn totally without support.

"You're right!" Ginger said, her voice now cheerful. "We both need a fresh start."

"You'll move too?" Autumn asked, a big smile growing on her face.

Ginger wanted to work somewhere she would be able to work in peace, without all the problems she was experiencing at AMC. She could no longer in good conscience remain where she was, and Autumn was right—fighting the system all by herself wouldn't do her any good. She felt herself breathe easier at the idea of moving to Washington.

Ginger smiled and nodded. "Wait until I tell my brother!"

CHAPTER 14

Seattle, Washington
April 11, 2020

"When was the last time you talked to her brother?" Dr. Khan asked Hyun as she stared down at Ginger's unmoving form.

"Yesterday morning. He has us call him every morning," Hyun replied.

"I see."

Dr. Porter was busy assessing Ginger's amputated legs for the last time before he signed off on Ginger's case. When he finished, he straightened up with a brisk nod.

"The surgical site looks great! Her legs are healing well without any signs of complication."

The other doctors looked relieved as he delivered his final sign-off opinion. Still, there was a lot of tension in the room. Hyun continued her work with the ECMO, while Clara collected Ginger's latest set of vital signs.

It was harder for Hyun to keep an eye on Clara when the doctors were crowded in the room with them. That made her even more anxious, and this morning was worse. Clara usually smelled of alcohol and cigarettes by lunchtime, but this morning,

Clara had shown up twenty minutes late and strongly reeking of both. Her hands were also shaking.

Hyun kept glancing at the doctors. It was hard to tell if they had noticed anything based on their unflinching facial expressions.

"It's been four weeks since the first dose of Actemra," Dr. Lee said. "I think we should go ahead and give her the second dose now."

"Sure, let's go ahead and try it," Dr. Khan agreed. Her fingers moved over the computer keyboard. "Okay, I just ordered the Actemra. Let's call her brother and sister-in-law. I'll explain it to them."

As soon as Daehan and Mary answered the call, Clara handed the screen to Dr. Khan. The doctor frowned at her, but then quickly forced a small smile for Daehan and Mary's benefit.

"What's happening, Doctor?" Daehan asked, his voice fearful.

Hyun's heart went out to the couple. She knew they were expecting more bad news, and she couldn't blame them. Ever since Ginger's leg amputation, Daehan and Mary had been hypersensitive about the calls coming from the doctors. That, coupled with the statistics and the general hysteria in the news, made it no wonder that they were bracing for the worst.

"The surgery sites are healing nicely. We had her start physical therapy right after the surgery to promote the range of motion and prevent additional blood clots in her legs," Dr. Khan said, leading with the good news.

"But?" Daehan asked, obviously bracing himself.

"The first dose of Actemra we administered four weeks ago wasn't effective. At this time, it's safe to give her a second dose, and that's what we're going to be doing."

"Given that the first dose didn't work, what are the odds that the second one will?" Mary asked, her voice nearly as strained as Daehan's.

"It's hard to say, but this is the best treatment option we have at this time," Dr. Khan said. "As you know, data about this disease is still inconclusive in many areas. We'll know if the second dose of Actemra is making a difference in a week or so."

"I see," Daehan said, sounding weary. It had been a long road, and the truth was that there was still a long way to go.

Dr. Khan wrapped up her part of the call and handed the screen to Clara, who began her ritual of reciting information and letting them talk to Ginger.

"May I see you in the hall?" Dr. Khan said quietly to Hyun.

Hyun nodded and followed her out of the room.

Dr. Khan glanced around and then lowered her voice. "Has she been drinking today?" She nodded toward Clara.

"I can't answer that question, but I do see all the indications that she has been drinking."

Dr. Khan swore under her breath. "How often does this happen?"

"Every day."

"Has it been affecting her work?"

Hyun hesitated a moment, wanting to choose her words carefully. "I can't be certain if her mistakes are directly caused by the drinking."

Dr. Khan rolled her eyes.

"Our manager shut me down when I tried to talk to her about it, but she might pay attention if you do," Hyun replied.

"Let's help her. She's already on probation, and we don't need any slip-ups, particularly not when she's caring for one of our sick patients."

"She's on probation?" Hyun asked, frowning.

Dr. Khan looked at her like she was crazy. "You didn't know? I'm surprised you weren't aware!"

"No one informed me of that," Hyun said, trying not to let her frustration show.

There was no way her manager had overlooked sharing that information with her. For the sake of the patients' safety, her manager should have warned her in some form, even if she was obligated to keep Clara's personal matter confidential. Hyun was just grateful she had kept a close eye on all of Clara's nursing tasks.

"Well, whatever the case, we need to get her sobered up," Dr. Khan said. "I'm going to do my best that she attend the detox program, but I'm unsure how far my voice will go since she is the daughter of one of our hospital board members. But we can't let any of our patients' care be affected by her drinking habit."

Dr. Khan walked off. Hyun went back into Ginger's room, just in time to have Clara hand her the screen.

Smiling at Daehan and Mary at that moment was one of the hardest things Hyun had ever had to do in her career, compounded by her stress from the mandatory overtime, wearing a non-hospital-grade respirator, the eye shield, and babysitting Clara.

Kirkland, Washington
October 2009

Ginger excitedly walked into Pine Health Hospital for her new job. Everything felt new, in fact. She and Autumn had just relocated from Alaska. They hadn't been able to get jobs working at the same hospital, but they were still close, within twenty miles of each other.

Ginger had been able to buy a two-bedroom house just two blocks away from Daehan and Mary in Kirkland. Autumn purchased a three-bedroom condo within walking distance from the Alderwood Medical Center, where she would be working at their Psych Department.

Pine Health was large, modern, and everything seemed fresh and clean.

Ginger looked around PHH's ED during the hospital-wide orientation, and a small picture frame caught her eye. It was an 8x12 frame, hung on the wall by the ambulance entrance, and it said, "Accredited for Trauma Level 4." She felt slightly relieved after reading this, since Angels Medical Center was Trauma Level 2. The closer an ED was to Level 1, the sicker the patients, and the more frequently chaotic events occurred. Since Ginger used to work in Level 2, her first thought was that working at PHH would be a piece of cake.

Here I'll be able to make a fresh start, she thought confidently.

Ginger began her job working the night shift. She would have preferred day shifts, but she was fine with starting at night.

On her first shift, Ginger walked toward the front desk. She'd taken no more than a dozen steps when she was intercepted by an older Japanese woman. The woman had an "RN" tag on her stethoscope, which she'd placed across her neck, but Ginger didn't see a nametag because it was flipped and showed only the back part of her badge.

"You must be Ginger," the woman said, extending her hand.

"Yes, how did you know?" Ginger asked.

"They told me you were Asian."

"Korean," Ginger said, somewhat taken aback.

"Great. That makes three of us. One from Japan, one from Pakistan, and now one from Korea."

"I'm sorry, I don't quite—"

"Understand?" the woman said, with a slight note of sarcasm in her voice. "Don't worry, you will. Until then, I've been assigned to show you around. Make sure you're…comfortable."

"I'm Ginger," Ginger said, trying to get her new colleague to introduce herself.

"Yes, we've established that."

"And what is your name?" Ginger said, giving up on trying to be subtle.

"Fuyo."

The woman turned on her heel and started walking. Ginger followed along as Fuyo gave her a brief orientation tour.

"You'll be working with about two-hundred nurses, thirty technicians, and twenty doctors. Not all at once, but that's the rough estimation of our entire staff here," Fuyo said as they walked through the ED.

As they walked, a few people they passed said hello or nodded. The majority, however, just ignored them.

"Most days, though it doesn't feel like it, you'll find we're very fast-paced here," Fuyo said.

That statement was evident in the brisk movements of the nurses around them. There was an air of urgency and intensity to everyone.

Ginger and Fuyo walked by two police officers who were waiting outside a room, their faces grim.

"You've come on a busy night. In addition to the standard broken bones, heart attacks, bites, and fevers, we've got a domestic violence stabbing and a rape victim," Fuyo said.

They kept walking. Fuyo paused for a moment at one door in a quiet corridor located a bit further away from the hectic scene from which they'd just emerged. Fuyo's face twisted in a scowl as she gazed at the door.

"This is the doctors' sleeping room, which they use on long shifts if they need rest. But trust me on this—do not just walk in there. Knock loudly first and wait about half a minute. And if a doctor ever invites you in there, just say no," Fuyo said firmly.

"What?" Ginger replied, bewildered.

Fuyo looked at her and sighed. "Several of the doctors use that bed frequently, but it's rarely for sleeping."

"Oh," Ginger said in realization. She felt a chill go through her.

"Moving on," Fuyo said, heading back down the hall at a rapid pace.

Ginger hurried to keep up. They stopped by the breakroom, where the department orientation was coming to a close. There, Ginger met a Pakistani nurse named Pari. Pari seemed very friendly, so it was a bit of a puzzle to Ginger why the woman was sitting by herself at a table.

Finally, they checked in with Mark, Ginger's new manager. Fuyo chose to wait outside in the hall while Ginger spoke with Mark.

Once Ginger sat down in Mark's office, he didn't look up from the papers he was perusing for a full two minutes. She shifted uncomfortably in her seat, wondering if she should volunteer to come back later.

Finally, he glanced up at her for a moment, then returned his attention to the papers on his desk.

"I expect you to get along with everyone. I don't appreciate troublemakers," he said without preamble.

Startled by his brusqueness, Ginger asked, "What do you mean?"

"I wasn't consulted in your hiring. The only reason you're here is because our hospital has to satisfy the EEOC requirement."

Ginger sat mutely, not sure how to respond.

"You can go now," he said dismissively.

Ginger stood, her head spinning. She made it back to the hallway as fast as she could.

Fuyo must have been able to see from Ginger's expression that it hadn't gone well. "You okay?"

"Is he like that with everyone?" Ginger asked.

"No, just the lucky few of us."

What in the world have I gotten myself into? Ginger wondered, but she tried to push the frightening thought out of her mind. Mark was probably just having a bad day, or maybe he was tough with all the new nurses until they proved themselves.

That morning, when she got off work, Ginger drove to Autumn's house. It was early still, but she knew Autumn would be up.

Ginger texted Autumn from the driveway so she wouldn't risk waking up the twins by ringing the doorbell or knocking. At seeing Autumn opening the door, Ginger got out of the car and entered the house. Autumn led her into the kitchen, where she handed Ginger a warm water.

"Sorry, I'm out of chamomile tea," Autumn said apologetically.

"This is fine," Ginger said, gratefully accepting the warm water.

Autumn poured herself a cup, and they both sat at the kitchen table.

"How was your first night?" Autumn asked.

"Awkward," Ginger admitted.

"What happened?"

"I think I got off on the wrong foot with my manager, Mark."

"That's rough. He'll come around when he sees what an exceptional nurse and a fabulous person you are," Autumn said encouragingly.

"I hope so."

"What else?" Autumn asked.

"All night, I couldn't get a single tech to help me with my patients."

"Were they short-staffed?" Autumn asked with a frown.

"They didn't seem to be. I saw them all over the place."

"Maybe they're nervous about working with a new hire. They don't know what you'll expect."

"Or maybe they're hazing the new hire," Ginger said. "But that doesn't make sense, because it's really the patients they're hurting."

"Do what I'm going to do when I start my job next week," Autumn offered.

"What's that?"

"Give them donuts. Donuts always break the ice."

"That would be a lot of donuts," Ginger remarked.

"Then bake cookies. You can whip up a few dozen. They'll love you for it. Take a few plates for the breakroom and tape a note saying you're looking forward to getting to know and work with everyone."

"That's a good idea," Ginger admitted.

"I do occasionally have them," Autumn said, grinning.

Ginger took a sip of her water and let the hot liquid warm her through and through.

"How are the boys doing with their classes?" she asked.

Autumn frowned. "The therapy classes the expert recommended turned out to be 150 dollars per hour for both boys to attend every session. Insurance doesn't cover it, so that all has to come out of my pocket. I signed them up for OT and speech therapy twice a week. In the end, it's going to come to 2,400 dollars a month."

"Can you afford that?" Ginger asked, alarmed.

"No. Even if I can pick up extra shifts, it's not going to work out. So at the end of the month, I'll take them out of OT and just keep speech therapy."

"I'm sorry," Ginger said sympathetically.

Autumn blinked her building tears away. "When I moved down here, I had a lot of hope. Do you think I expected too much? I had no idea how expensive all the therapies would be." Autumn broke down and began to cry in earnest. "At this point, I'm just hoping their school is good."

Ginger hugged Autumn and told her, "I do believe you have a legitimate concern as a mom. All parents want the best for their children. I know there's no federal funding, but have you researched whether there's state funding for autistic children?"

Autumn nodded.

"And?"

"There isn't any."

Ginger found she was speechless. All she could do was hug Autumn warmly before leaving her house.

For Ginger's next shift, she did as Autumn suggested. She brought in chocolate chip cookies to the staff breakroom, hoping to break the ice with her new coworkers. People seemed to gravitate toward them, which pleased her instantly.

An hour later, she went back into the breakroom, trying to find a tech to help with her patient. She noticed that nearly half the cookies were gone, but so was the little note introducing herself that she had put by the cookies. With dismay, she discovered that someone had crumpled it up and thrown it on the floor next to the garbage can.

Pari came into the room.

"What's wrong?" Pari asked, noticing Ginger's crestfallen expression.

Ginger pointed to the crumpled paper on the ground. "Who would do that?"

Pari shook her head. "Don't let it get you down. Some people are idiots. They're small and close-minded, and it would take a miracle to change that."

CHAPTER 15

Seattle, Washington
April 19, 2020

"It's a miracle," Dr. Khan said, staring in disbelief at the chart.

"Tell us," Dr. Lee prodded.

Dr. Khan glanced at Clara and nodded to her.

"Her vital signs are stabilized. BP 110/60, heart rate 78 with sinus rhythm. The urine output is also normal, 750 ml in the past 12 hours," Clara said, unable to keep the excitement out of her voice.

"Her gas level has also normalized," Tom the RT reported.

Dr. Khan smiled. "Based on the lab results, I think we can have the trialing off ECMO starting with a few minutes. What are your thoughts from the cardiac standpoint, Dr. Lim?"

"Based on her new ECHO results, her heart function has improved to close to normal. This is as good as it gets for a post-MI patient. I think her heart is strong enough to take on the full load. I'm all for it," she said.

"Thank you, Dr. Lim. What about you, Dr. Ortiz? I would like to hear your opinion on her pulmonary status," Dr. Khan said, turning to address the pulmonologist.

"She is hemodynamically stable, her chest X-ray is looking good, and the blood gas also is within normal limits. I think she is ready for it."

"Great! Thank you all for your valuable input. I'll call Daehan and Mary, and let them know about our plan," Dr. Khan said excitedly.

The other doctors shuffled out of the room, and Dr. Khan turned to Hyun. "As discussed, let's start trialing off the ECMO with a few seconds to minutes. I'll type in these orders. Let's touch base at the end of the day."

"Sounds great!" Hyun said enthusiastically. Hyun knew this was a big moment. It felt like Ginger had finally turned the corner and was on the road to getting well.

Dr. Khan spoke excitedly as she talked to Daehan and Mary, which communicated itself to the couple, who in turn started speaking more rapidly, their voices almost breathless.

After the video call was over and Dr. Khan left to see other patients, Hyun took a moment to refocus. Trialing off the ECMO was a big step, and it would mean a lot if Ginger could be completely off the machine.

Hyun flipped the ECMO switch and held her breath.

At the end of her shift, Hyun tracked down Dr. Khan. The doctor stared at her blankly for a moment as though she was trying to gather her thoughts.

"Ginger? The ECMO?" Hyun patiently reminded Dr. Khan, who was dealing with more patients than Hyun. It was clear that the twelve-hour shifts and the madness of the current hospital situation was taking a toll on everyone.

"Right. How did it go?" Dr. Khan asked.

"Very well. In fact, I feel optimistic that Ginger is ready for an eight-hour trial off."

"That's fantastic! Let's do that tomorrow morning, starting at eight a.m. sharp! That will be the best time since we'll have all the specialists available and the hospital will be running in full gear, just in case things don't go well."

Hyun nodded. It would definitely be the best time to try such a crucial task. Plus, she wouldn't have felt comfortable if they'd started the process during the end of her shift, when she would leave and hand it over to the night shift.

"Good work, Hyun," Dr. Khan said. "I'll see you in the morning."

Kirkland, Washington
September 2010

Ginger and Pari met up in the breakroom for lunch. When Ginger sat down, it was obvious to her that Pari was upset about something.

"Are you okay?" Ginger asked as she opened up her lunch, a pre-made salad from Costco.

"Do I look okay?" Pari asked.

"No, which is why I'm asking."

Pari sighed. "I didn't get the house supervisor position."

Ginger was stunned. "What? Why not? You have such strong qualifications, and you have leadership skills, a wealth of knowledge, and you're kind to everyone, even the most difficult patients. You would have made a fabulous house supervisor."

"I know, but apparently, twenty years of nursing experience in ED, ICU, PCU, OR, and day surgery isn't good enough," Pari said glumly.

"How can it not be?" Ginger asked as she poured dressing over her salad. "I mean, what else would you need to get that job?"

"I'd need to be white," Pari said bluntly.

Ginger looked at her in surprise. "You are white."

Pari's jaw twitched. "Apparently not white enough. Pakistanis are considered Caucasian for legal and census purposes, but that doesn't mean we're treated that way."

"Oh, Pari, I'm so sorry!" Ginger said, her heart breaking for her friend. "Who did Mark end up promoting?"

"Nana."

Ginger nearly dropped her fork. "Nana? Nana! She's a new hire. Her only previous nursing experience was one year in an operating room."

"Yeah, well, apparently that's all you need as long as your skin's the right color and you don't have an accent."

Ginger was outraged. "I can't believe they'd do that to you!"

Pari shrugged. "I can. Look what they did to you."

"What they did to me?" Ginger asked, confused.

"Remember last month when I submitted that proposal to Mark to make you an ED IV instructor and resource nurse? I emailed him saying what an asset you are to our department and how you help speed up our care and prevent delay, which is often caused by the other nurses' poor IV skills."

"It was very kind of you to do that," Ginger said.

"Kind nothing. It was the truth. Everyone comes to you when they have difficulty placing an IV on their patients. And more than half of our nurses are incompetent in that area. I'm still angry that Mark just dismissed it and emailed the whole staff to let them know it was a hard no from him."

"That was a bit awkward," Ginger admitted.

"You're too nice," Pari said, shaking her head.

Just then, Chase, one of the emergency room techs, walked into the breakroom. He stopped and sniffed the air dramatically.

"Yuck! What is that smell? So pungent!" He turned and looked at Ginger. "What horrible, smelly thing are you eating?"

Ginger stared at him in surprise. "An Italian-American vinaigrette salad from Costco."

"Well, it's awful. You shouldn't eat it in here and stink up the place."

"That's rude, and I think you're overreacting. I don't complain about your food, even when you reheat old anchovies in the microwave."

"Ignore him. He's a jerk," Pari said. "Clearly, he's allergic to Italian things."

"Hey, I am Italian," Chase said, scowling.

"Really? It must be hard going through life with an aversion to yourself," Pari said innocently.

Chase turned red in the face and took a step toward her.

"Forget it, Chase, they're not worth your time. Come sit here next to me," a voice purred.

Ginger looked and saw Lily batting her eyes at Chase. Chase's whole demeanor changed as he grinned back and went to sit with her.

"Lily should know better. Chase is married with two kids," Pari muttered under her breath.

"That doesn't seem to bother either of them. Thanks, by the way," Ginger said. It was out of character for Pari to engage with someone who was being antagonistic. It revealed to Ginger just how upset she was for being passed over.

Ginger sighed, shaking her head. "I'm sorry I'm bringing it up again, but it's difficult to accept the fact that Mark chose Nana over you. I can't wrap my head around it. Mark knows your qualifications. Besides, it's an easy decision because Nana is the complete opposite of who you are, from both a personal and professional standpoint—you are wise, she is not; you have the leadership skills, she doesn't; you have over twenty years of nursing experience, Nana only has one; and you are mature, while she's an immature spoiled brat."

"You've noticed that too?" Pari asked, raising her eyebrows.

Ginger shuddered at the memory. "Yes. The other day she was super rude to me in front of my patient. I had to ask her to leave the room, and I did so politely. However, the patient was also rude to me, as if she got permission from Nana to act that way. She looked at me from head to toe and began asking questions about where I was born, what school I went to, and how much experience I have—all while she was receiving my care!"

"They'd never have asked you that if you were white," Pari said, sipping her jasmine tea.

"It was so odd and frustrating. I kept my answers short and minimal, but it bothered me. Why didn't she ask me treatment-related questions instead? I felt like I was being interviewed or interrogated while I was helping her. Nana is a bad influence on our co-workers and our patients."

"Yes, and now she's become one of our house supervisors," Pari said.

Ginger had no other words to offer to her friend to make her feel better. All she could manage to say was, "It's their loss. Cheer up, Pari."

That night, when Ginger got home, the weight of everything that was wrong at work weighed heavily on her. Nothing she did could distract her from her anguish, so she finally decided to sit down and write to Eungi, though she felt more as though she was writing in her diary to herself, unloading all her feelings and thoughts.

Eungi,

So much for my relief when I first saw Trauma Level 4 sign in PHH ED. This place is corrupt and full of drama, not Trauma.

I am getting so frustrated. I try to get along with my co-workers. It is so challenging because they discriminate against the patients and me. You wouldn't believe half of what goes on around here. What's sad is that sometimes I'm not even shocked anymore by all the bad behavior I see. I need to put all this down so I can clear my head. I'm struggling with where to begin.

For starters, the ED techs neglect their work. Seriously! Pine Health Hospital's minimum qualification for hiring an Emergency Technician is a high school diploma, with no experience required. They train new techs from a few days to a couple of weeks. The new techs are given simple splinting classes, shown how to perform a 12-lead EKG, taught how to take vital signs, and other basic training. Techs are allowed to splint as long as it is a simple fracture, such as a hairline fracture, under a doctor's instruction. ED techs are permitted to take the patients for the "road test" (take the patient to walk around the hallway or take them to the bathroom) and report what they observed to the primary nurse or the doctor so as to determine the patient's discharge suitability. It's important work, but not that hard. Yet somehow, we only have three techs who perform their jobs professionally: Urban, Blessing, and Nash.

I think part of the problem is that most techs are hired because they have a prior connection to the hospital. Instead of trying to work hard, they abuse their family and friends' power. Worse yet, they pick and choose whom they want to help, and they give priority to the Caucasian nurses' patients. When it is a non-Caucasian nurse's patient, they either delay their tasks or simply disappear somewhere.

Remember that ED tech, Tony, I told you about? The one who asked me out? He's now making my life miserable because I said no. He chases after all the female nurses and techs. He's chubby and has a stubby mustache with curly gray hair. He has a horrible attitude, but he's the techs' union rep, so he thinks he has a ticket to be bad and no one can stop him.

Two weeks ago, he threw a used bloody IV line at me. I'm glad it didn't splash into my mouth or eyes. Can you believe that? He then said I made "too much of a mess" during patient care and threatened to report me to the manager. I told the charge nurse what happened. Maybe I shouldn't have, because now none of my patients can get tech care whenever he's on shift.

Last night, unfortunately, I found one of the places Tony disappears to. I was working the graveyard shift and I had to go down to the morgue with Pari. It's the tech's job to take bodies down there, but Tony wasn't around. As it turns out, he was already in the morgue…he was in there having sex with Melody.

Can you believe that? I don't know what's worse, that they're having sex at work or that they're disrespecting the dead that way. It made me so sick I wanted to throw up. Of course, nothing will probably happen to either of them.

Afterward, Pari told me that last month she caught Tony in there having sex with Nicole, another tech, and they weren't even reprimanded when she'd reported them.

I'm speechless how corrupt this place is, especially given that Nicole is also having an affair with Dr. Koppel. They have sex in the doctor's sleeping quarters and she doesn't even try to be subtle about it. She's constantly giving him neck and shoulder massages in front of everyone in ED. She thinks it entitles her to bully the rest of us, and that makes it okay for her to not do her tech duty. She gets aggressive and verbally abusive every time I try to give her a task. I've reported her to the charge nurse and the managers, but I've never heard from either of them. Her affair with Dr. Koppel is making him negligent in his work too.

Last week, a patient arrived at 3 a.m. in an ambulance. It had been quiet before then. No one could find Dr. Koppel, so several of us started looking for him. Unfortunately, I was the one who found him in the doctors' sleeping quarters. You guessed it…

he and Nicole were too busy having sex to worry about someone dying.

Unfortunately, these stories are not the worst ones I have. Remember, there are only three techs who actually do their job without causing problems? That's three out of the thirty we have!

Alana also has sex at work with Dr. MacIntosh. At least, they do it in their cars. That's not all though. She and her friend, Salena, abuse drugs while sitting in their cars together. They'll vanish and come back with dilated pupils—completely high. It's obvious from the distinctive smell of marijuana and their constant laughter.

The other day, Pari and I caught Salena stealing Pari's patient's diamond ring. Pari reported the incident to Mark, but he didn't respond. Salena still works as a tech and continues stealing. Today, out of the blue, Mark sends me an email and asks me about one of my patient's gold chain. He described in detail how the necklace looked. He stated that the patient called him up and asked to find his missing necklace. Mark indicated the chain was a "big bald eagle, pure 3oz gold", which I saw in Salena's hands while she was going through the patient's belongings list. I was highly offended by his email since he was implying that I had something to do with a missing necklace. I responded to him via email and told him that I saw the necklace in Salena's hands while she was going through my patient's belonging's list. I never received any response from Mark. Unfortunately, Salena still manages to steal items from our patients like a pro—she waits for a moment of chaos in the ED and pockets them. When *the patients ask about their jewelry, she tells them that they're "delirious" and need to rest, or she blames the primary nurse. Ever since Mark's email, I ask the charge to switch Salena with one of the better ones, or I just go through the list myself before she can get at them. It's disgraceful and shameful since I have to focus on the patient's belongings list instead of helping their medical needs. Everyone is saying Mark uses Salena to spy on all the staff. Perhaps that may be the reason why she is still allowed to work in ED. He's protecting her, while he should be protecting the patients.*

Ugh! Just writing about all the corruption in PHH is overwhelming!

Ginger went on to describe to Eungi what had happened with Pari's promotion and Chase's rudeness at lunch. The more she thought about it, the more she realized just how awful some of the techs had been to her. Adrik would refuse to handle any of the non-Caucasian nurses' patients, and Altin would only work with the Caucasian male nurses.

Most of the time, Ginger had to ignore it, except for when she cared for sick patients, for whom she would fight to the teeth so they received urgent medical treatment. As a result, the techs and nurses hated Ginger's guts.

It gave her a headache just thinking about all of it. When she finally was able to stop writing and go to sleep, she tossed and turned all night.

CHAPTER 16

Seattle, Washington
April 20, 2020

Despite being exhausted, Hyun had barely slept all night. She woke in the early hours of the morning, and when she couldn't fall back asleep, she forced herself to get up.

Today was a big day, as it was Ginger's "ECMO weaning-off day." She'd been watching over her patient for almost six weeks now. That, in itself, was unusual. Then again, everything was so unusual these days that crazy had somehow become the new normal.

The news on television was too depressing, so she turned it off. Her drive to work had now become super short, with basically no traffic on the roads. It was eerie, and she couldn't help but feel as though she was living in a ghost town. That is, until she arrived at the hospital, where she became part of the busy medical team battling COVID and trying to save patients' lives.

Joe, the night ECMO RN, was waiting for her at the nurses' station when she arrived at the ICU.

"I hear you're looking to put me out of a job today," he said jokingly, with a big smile as he gazed at Ginger through the glass barrier from the nurses' station. Hyun hadn't seen him smile in weeks.

"It's about time!" she told him with a smile to match his own. "At least, where one patient is concerned."

"Man, Ginger has been through it all," he said, his smile slipping a little.

"I know, but at least it looks like she's going to recover."

"We need good news around here. They're calling her a miracle. I think you've had a lot to do with that."

"And you," she said to him, meaning it.

He shrugged. "We do what we can."

She nodded in agreement.

Joe continued, "We made sure that we infused Dobutamine all night through her central line. She tolerated it beautifully."

"Good, good!" Hyun said, giving him a thumbs up. The drug was used to increase and improve Ginger's cardiac output.

Joe gave her a few more updates before leaving the station. By quarter to eight, Hyun made her way into Ginger's room. She sat quietly next to Ginger for several minutes, talking to the unconscious woman before the doctors arrived.

Clara was the last into the room, panting and sweating profusely as she walked in. Despite wearing a respirator, her alcohol stench was even more noticeable than usual, and Hyun saw Dr. Khan narrow her eyes disapprovingly.

Dr. Khan, Dr. Lim, and Dr. Ortiz stood at Ginger's right-hand side. The ECHO technician stood at Ginger's left-hand side with the machine to reassess the function of her heart. Clara stood between the IV pole and the cardiac monitor to measure and collect Ginger's blood pressure under the doctor's order. Hyun was near the end of Ginger's bed in the right-hand corner, close to the ECMO, and she was still able to view the ECHO monitor.

There were four different stages to go through with the ECMO weaning-off process.

The ECHO tech began his task by placing a wand on Ginger's left side of her chest with plenty of gel. He moved on to measuring the blood volume of the right and left ventricles of her heart. Both her heart activity and her baseline blood volume on the right and left ventricles were displayed on the ECHO screen.

Dr. Lim turned to everyone in the room. "Shall we get started?" Everyone gave her a thumbs up. With that, Dr. Lim nodded to Hyun and ordered, "Gradually decrease the ECMO flow."

Hyun slowly decreased the flow in increments of .5 liters a minute to half the original rate. Everyone in the room held their breath and monitored Ginger's hemodynamic responses. At the same time, Hyun followed Dr. Lim's order on volume challenge and reduced the ECMO flow to its minimum rate. Three doctors' eyes were glued on Ginger, the ECHO monitor, and the cardiac monitor to assess the response of her heart and her blood pressure.

"She's tolerating it well so far," Dr. Lim cautiously remarked.

"Infuse her with 5% albumin," Dr. Lim ordered Clara.

Clara hurried to do so, her hands shaking so badly that for a moment, Hyun thought someone else would have to take over. Her own heart began pounding at the sight. Carrying out Dr. Lim's order marked a crucial moment, and if Clara messed up, it could cause a serious problem.

Finally, Dr. Khan had enough. "Go find someone else to do this," she snapped at Clara.

Clara shuffled and hurried out of the room. She returned a minute later with Meena—Clara all but shoving Meena into the room before disappearing.

Meena briskly went to the sink and washed her hands. She came back over and administered the drug. Hyun met Meena's eyes, and gave her a grateful look.

Meena seemed to understand, nodding slowly at Hyun.

"I'm very pleased with the results so far," Dr. Lim told everyone with a satisfied smile. "We'll continue to assess LV and RV function during infusion of dobutamine for the next six hours."

Once the doctors had cleared out of the room, Hyun turned to Meena.

"Thank you," she said.

Meena shook her head. "I'm glad I was here to help."

Hyun was on her own for the rest of the day. She didn't know where Clara was, but suspected she might have gone home. It was just as well. Clara wasn't in any condition to be treating patients.

At the end of her shift, Hyun met with Dr. Khan, Joe, Matthew, and the night RT Abigail, who were all back for the evening shift.

"Dr. Lim has concluded that Ginger's LV and RV functions have recovered," Dr. Khan said. "I want to monitor Ginger for another twelve hours on the vent without being assisted by the ECMO."

Joe and Abigail nodded. It would be their responsibility to make sure things went well during their shift.

"If she tolerates it well throughout the night, I'm planning on having the surgeon remove the circuit line before extubating her," Dr. Khan explained.

"Sounds great!" Hyun said, giving a thumb's up with her right hand.

"Good. I'll see you all in the morning," Dr. Khan said, walking away slowly.

"You get all the fun stuff," Joe teased Hyun lightly.

"Hopefully, we just get to babysit," said Abigail.

"I hope babysitting tonight is boring," Hyun responded.

"Me too," Joe, Matthew and Abigail said simultaneously, but their facial expressions were somber.

Kirkland, Washington
February 27, 2016

Ginger had been working for more than six years at Pine Health Hospital. She had since switched to the day shift, working from 9 a.m. to 9 p.m. The management had changed because of a scandal involving failure to provide 100% of their staff's breaks for several years.

Unfortunately, her new manager, Gerry, was as bad as Mark had been. Ginger had tried to grow a thick skin and not let things get to her, but it was hard.

Just a few months earlier, after Pari and Ginger had filed a racial discrimination report, Gerry got Pari's daughter fired. The young woman had worked as a unit secretary in the ED for three years and had an exemplary record. When she asked why she was being let go, Gerry told her, "You are not being terminated. We are eliminating your position due to a budget issue. By the way, your mother holds the best answer to your questions. She'll know what I mean."

Gerry's words had been a warning to Pari. Even worse, Gerry contradicted herself by hiring someone else in Pari's daughter's position. At the same time, neither the hospital nor the union ever followed up on Pari and Ginger's discrimination reports. It had all become so frustrating and discouraging, Ginger had given up pushing further.

Some days, the struggle was more challenging than others. Today, Ginger was at the end of her 12-hour shift, and she was exhausted because she'd only had a 15-minute break throughout her entire shift. She kept waiting for a nurse to show up and relieve her so she could go home. Ginger waited for her relief nurse for half an hour, but no one came to take the report from her. Ginger approached the charge nurse's desk and asked for the relief nurse.

The charge nurse, George, sighed and said, "We are short on nurses again. I'll take the report."

"I can stay until the patient gets picked up. He has scheduled to get picked up within an hour, but, as you know, the medics might not appear on time since it's Saturday."

"I know, but I can't. I'll get in big trouble if I let you stay. You know how it is. Gerry is obsessed with the budget. Just give me the report. I'll deal with it."

"Okay then, here it is. The patient is in Trauma Room 5. He is a bilateral, above-the-knee amputee. He has been medically cleared and he is eating dinner, and it's his second serving. You should know that instead of using the call button, he yells out. The entire ED can hear him when he does, so you won't miss him when he asks for help. As I mentioned, he's just waiting to be picked up by the medics."

"It's a good thing his room is just a few feet away from me. We all can keep an eye on him," George said. "Now get out of here."

"All right." Ginger grabbed her things, then found Dr. Green.

"Is it time for you to go home, Ginger?" Dr. Green asked.

"Yes. I'm going home. George assumed care on T5."

"Okay, thanks for your help. Good night," he replied.

It had been a long shift that day. All Ginger could think about was going home, taking a long, hot shower and having a bite to eat before she collapsed in bed. That thought had been the only thing that had gotten her through the last two hours.

But when she reached her car, she realized she had five missed calls from Autumn, which was unusual.

Autumn had left three voicemails, the first two of which said, "Call me" and the third one was a bit longer: "I'm sorry. I've been going out of my mind with worry over here. When you get off work, could you come over? I need you."

Ginger hastily texted her, letting her know she was on her way. Her stomach did flip-flops during the entire drive between the hospital and Autumn's house as she wondered what had gone so badly for her friend.

When she arrived, she texted Autumn from the driveway as usual. Autumn threw open the door, clearly having been hovering near it while she was waiting for her.

Ginger quickly got out of her car and hurried up the walk. Autumn threw her arms around her and sobbed.

"Are the boys okay?" Ginger asked with trepidation.

"I don't know."

"What's wrong?"

"They're asleep now. They're safe upstairs."

Ginger ended up guiding Autumn into the kitchen, where two cups of hot chocolate were already sitting on the table. Autumn saved hot chocolate for really bad days, so Ginger's concern skyrocketed even more.

They sat at the table, and Ginger wrapped her hands around the mug and carefully observed her friend. Autumn slowly pulled herself together, reaching for her mug. She picked it up and took a sip.

"You want to tell me what's going on?" Ginger asked.

"You remember two weeks ago when you picked Noah and Liam up from school, and they had those bruises on their arms?"

"Yes."

"Well, it's happened three more times since then, and the last two times they've had bruises on their torso as well."

"Oh my gosh! Why didn't you tell me?" Ginger asked, dismayed.

"I wasn't sure what was going on. Well, today, I sent them to school with little miniature security cameras on their shirts. I found the cameras online. I was planning to review the videos and see if I could figure out how they were getting hurt."

That was sensible on Autumn's part. The twins were almost seventeen, but they still had a communication problem, having the mental age of three. They were virtually non-verbal and only able to say a few words here and there.

"That's smart. Really good idea."

"Thanks. I saw someone else talking about it in an online support group. Well, before lunch, I got called down to the school by Susanna, the principal. She didn't tell me on the phone what it was about. I got there and found Liam and Noah in the office along with their teacher, Tucker."

Autumn took a long sip of hot chocolate, and Ginger noticed that her hands were shaking so hard that Autumn sloshed a bit of the beverage onto her shirt. She didn't even seem to notice.

"I walked past Tucker, and I could actually smell the alcohol on his breath."

"You can tell by looking at his face that he's an alcoholic and he's causing his body a lot of harm," Ginger said softly.

"And a lot more harm to his students. Susanna starts going on and on about what a good teacher Tucker is and how much he cares about the disabled students. I finally asked her to get to the point. According to her, Noah and Liam have a problem with authority. She said they refused to follow Tucker's instructions and were disrespectful to him. Because of that, she's suspending both of them."

"That's outrageous! Noah and Liam are both good boys," Ginger exclaimed.

"I did my best not to lose it right there on the spot. I told her I would talk to her tomorrow, then I got myself and the boys out of there. I wanted to have a chance to review the videos before I gave my response."

Autumn paused to take another sip of hot chocolate.

"What did you see?" Ginger asked.

"Nothing yet. I have it all loaded up on my laptop, but...but...I didn't want to watch it alone," she said, tears springing to her eyes.

Ginger hugged her fiercely. "You don't have to."

"Thank you. I knew you'd understand."

Autumn set up the laptop on the kitchen table, and she and Ginger scooted their chairs next to each other so they could watch the video together. They started with Liam's camera.

At first, there was nothing too interesting. Autumn even fast-forwarded through some of it. Then she found what she was looking for.

They both leaned in to watch. Tucker was sitting at the head of the room with his feet on his desk. They saw his teacher's aid working with another student in the far corner of the room. Tucker called Noah up to his desk, and Noah obeyed. The camera got closer to them, indicating that Liam had shuffled forward to stay close to his brother.

Tucker had taped off the floor around his desk with black and yellow crime scene tape. Ginger had seen the tape before when she'd visited the classroom. She found it offensive and far from "educational." Autumn had asked Tucker to remove the tape at the beginning of the school year, but Tucker had refused, saying, "I'm just trying to teach kids the meaning of boundaries." Autumn didn't want to make it into a huge deal, so she let it go. Ginger agreed with Autumn that there were better ways than crime-scene tape to teach kids about boundaries.

Noah had stopped next to the desk, standing on top of the tape.

"Outside the tape!" Tucker barked.

Noah just stood there, frozen and shaking.

"Listen to me! Outside the tape!" Tucker yelled and pushed at Noah's feet with his wooden pointer.

Noah stepped back an inch, but he was still standing over the crime tape. It was clear he didn't understand what the teacher wanted.

Tucker yanked his legs off the desk and lashed out again with his wooden pointer. He poked Noah hard in the belly with it. "Back!" he shouted.

Noah jumped, startled, and began to cry.

Tucker jabbed the pointer into Noah's forehead. On the tape, they could hear Liam making little moaning sounds of distress as he watched what was happening to his brother.

"You stupid bastard!" Tucker shouted.

Noah turned and ran for the door to escape the classroom. Tucker chased after him and grabbed his wrist, twisting it hard. Noah struggled in Tucker's grip and bit his hand.

"You son of a bitch!" Tucker screamed as he let go of Noah.

The video image started rocking from side to side as Liam clearly struggled to come to terms with what was happening.

Noah began to cry harder, and the fear on his face was heartbreaking. With nowhere to escape, he lay down on the floor and curled up in a fetal position. He began rocking himself, then suddenly, he began to seize.

Liam's moaning on the video turned into wailing as he clearly grew terrified for his twin.

Tucker let out a long string of profanity, then pulled out his phone. "Susanna? One of the stupid twins is having seizures. How am I supposed to know which one? Yeah, last time, they just stopped after a few minutes."

He should be calling an ambulance, Ginger thought grimly.

Tucker hung up with the principal. He then turned and went back to his desk, where he sat down like nothing at all was happening.

The camera then seemed to zoom in on Noah as Liam ran over to him. Noah had seizures for five minutes before they finally stopped. A minute later, Tucker returned and loomed over both boys.

"Get up. We're going to the principal's office," he said, his voice gruff.

With a shaking hand, Autumn stopped the tape. "I'm going to kill him," she whispered, her voice raw with pain and rage.

Ginger shared Autumn's anger and outrage. She quietly put her hand on Autumn's shoulder, "This is terrible. I'm so sorry."

"First things first. Tomorrow I'm going to the neurologist, and then I'm getting a lawyer. These people are evil criminals. I will see to it that they never work in a school setting again."

"You have my full support," Ginger said solemnly.

After comforting Autumn for a few more minutes, Ginger made it home and got some sleep. When she woke, she had breakfast and then checked her email. She had one from Pari, and clicked on it. Her blood ran cold as she read it.

Hi Ginger,

I just want you to know that after you went home, your patient in T5, Mr. West, yelled out, "I have to poop! Help me!" I was in the middle of care for one of my patients, so, I asked Anna, the unit secretary, to page George. It turns out George wasn't able to help Mr. West because he was busy breaking a nurse who hadn't had a break for 8 hours. According to Anna: "George told me, 'I'm busy covering a nurse's break. Just ignore him.'"

Mr. West kept on yelling, "Help me! Fuck! I have to poop!" He even threatened, "I'm just gonna poop here if you don't help me!"

Ginger, I could hear Mr. West yelling, even in my patient's room. I poked my head out. I saw Adrik and Salena, just sitting around and playing with their cell phones. I asked them to help Mr. West. Do you know what they told me? "We need to take our break," and they disappeared, completely ignoring me and Mr. West's urgent yelling.

Dr. Green also dismissed Mr. West's cries for help. He said, "What a dick, yelling out like that!" Then he disappeared.

I finally went to T5 after I had finished helping my patient. Mr. West said, "I already went in my pants." The patient was able to turn, so I was able to clean him up by myself.

About an hour later, Lily took over care from George. Mr. West complained to Lily about his pooping his pants because no one helped him. Mr. West told Lily that I had cleaned him up. Lily got excited about the incident, but she wasn't interested in who helped him out.

After Lily discharged Mr. West, she told everyone about the patient defecating himself in bed because you, Ginger, didn't help him. I said to Lily, "It wasn't Ginger's fault. She wasn't even around."

However, Lily didn't listen. She told everyone she is writing you up.

Let's get together and talk about this,

Pari

Ginger reread the email three times, utterly stunned. She emailed Pari back and took a shower, struggling to clear her head. She knew Lily didn't like her, but she was shocked to hear that she was blatantly lying about her.

Ginger spent the rest of her day off fretting, as there were too many thoughts crowding her head.

On Monday morning, Ginger got dressed and headed to work, worried about what she was facing after Pari's report. As soon as she set foot in her department, she was called into Gerry's office.

On reaching the office, Ginger sat down. Without greeting her, Gerry glared at Ginger across her desk. "You went home without cleaning Mr. West. You cannot go home without cleaning your patient's poop!"

"He didn't poop or even need to poop on my shift. All of that happened afterward," Ginger said, trying to stay collected. "He was eating dinner when I left. I provided him the best care possible while he was my responsibility."

"That's not what Lily says in this report," Gerry said, tapping her nails on a piece of paper on her desk. "And she's not the only one complaining about you."

"Who has anything bad they could possibly say about me?" Ginger blurted out. "I do my job, and I do it well. If you are truly concerned about the quality care and safety issues, I'd like to hear your plans on how you would improve some of the issues that I mentioned on my last report."

That's when it hit her. Gerry and the other managers had been circling her like vultures for weeks. Every time Ginger tried to point out unfair or unsafe practices, her reports went ignored. She realized then that she was being ignored, and targeted.

"It's my responsibility to send this up the chain of command," Gerry said, a cruel smile touching her lips.

"It's a lie. Pari can tell you. She was working during all this, and she knows that Mr. West was yelling for help to go to the bathroom long after my shift was over, after I'd been sent home by George. No one would help him, so Pari was the one who cleaned him up."

"I don't care who cleaned him up. I just care about who didn't," Gerry snapped.

"But I wasn't here when it happened. If I had been, I would have helped him go in the first place. Ask Pari."

"I don't care what that Paki trash thinks or says. I have a report from Lily, a good nurse, who has earned the trust and respect of her peers."

Ginger was deeply offended for Pari, but kept her mouth shut.

"Get out of here and back to work while you still can," Gerry said.

Ginger stood up, hands clenched at her sides, and it took every ounce of her willpower not to tell Gerry exactly what she thought of her and Lily.

She went through the rest of her day in a kind of haze. When she finally had a chance to speak with Pari, she freely expressed her outrage and concern.

"What are you going to do?" Pari asked.

"I don't know what I can do," Ginger said, feeling anxious and stressed.

When her shift ended, Ginger went home. She spent a sleepless night worrying about what else might result from Lily's lies.

In the morning, when she went back to work, she was called into the HR office.

Ginger walked toward the office. On her way, she saw Gerry walk out of the ED supply room, holding a gray walking boot in her hand. Ginger was confused by the sight, but didn't think too much of it.

She arrived in the HR lobby, and was told to take a seat and wait for a few minutes before she could see Bill, the hospital's attorney. After a few minutes, the receptionist told her to go in.

As Ginger stood up, she spotted Gerry coming out of the nearby restroom. On her right foot, she wore the gray walking boot she had been carrying minutes earlier, and she was walking with a pronounced limp that hadn't been there before.

Ginger walked into Bill's office, as she had been instructed by the receptionist. A moment later, Gerry followed Ginger inside.

"Hi, Bill," Gerry said, taking the seat right across from Bill's desk. Sitting next to her was Tami, the union representative.

"Oh no, Gerry! What happened to your leg?" Bill asked sympathetically.

"I fell last night. It's a hairline fracture. Luckily, it doesn't require surgery."

Ginger stared open-mouthed as Gerry rambled on with her lie.

"Here, let me get you a chair so you can prop up your leg," Bill said, rushing to move the other chair across from his desk into position. He carefully lifted Gerry's right leg and helped settle it onto the chair.

"Thank you, Bill, that's much better."

"It's no problem, no problem at all," Bill said with a smile.

Ginger stood there, wondering where she was going to sit now that Gerry had taken up the last chair for her leg. Finally, Bill looked at Ginger, as if noticing her presence for the first time. He frowned and pointed to the corner of the room.

"You can stand over there for now," he said.

Feeling outraged, Ginger froze and felt her face flush. It was an obvious intimidation tactic, and she hated that they were using it on her. But she made herself walk to the corner and stand, waiting for what was coming next.

"So let's get started," Bill said. "Ginger, you neglected your patient. You violated HIPAA by discussing Mr. West's case with your union representative via email. Because of these reasons, we're firing you. Sign here if you agree. We're going to escort you to the locker room so you can clean out your locker."

Before Ginger could get a word in, Bill jumped in again. "Gerry, I will escort her out. You save your leg."

"Thank you, Bill, that's very kind."

You're all liars and thieves and the worst kind of racists. That's what Ginger wanted to say. But before she could get anything out, Tami held up a hand.

"Save your words. Ginger. Don't say anything now."

"I'm not saying anything, or signing anything," Ginger said. She wanted to shout the words, but they came out as a mere whisper.

"Good girl," Tami said.

That was the last straw for Ginger. Tami was the union representative who was supposed to protect and represent Ginger in this matter. Instead, Tami was telling her to be quiet while the union did…what? It certainly didn't seem like they were advocating on her behalf. Why was she paying dues to the union if there was no help coming from that quarter? And now, Tami's patronizing manner toward her was intolerable.

Ginger wasn't a "good girl." She was a woman, a fantastic nurse, and she was being viciously and deliberately maligned. She wanted to yank the boot off Gerry's foot and tell the others that Gerry was lying about that as well. But knowing the people around her, they'd probably have her arrested for assault. And she had no doubt that at least one doctor at the hospital would lie to cover for Gerry.

Ginger pushed herself off the wall. "I'm going to the locker room myself. If you follow me, I will call all the local TV stations and tell them what led to this. Tell them the truth about all of you."

"I think going with her is too harsh. Let her go on her own," Tami said.

Though Bill agreed to not accompany her, Ginger felt completely humiliated as she walked to the locker room. She forced herself to keep her head high. She wasn't going to let anyone see her cower or grovel or cry. She fought back her tears with every step.

She walked by Pari, who looked upset. "I'm so sorry!" she burst out.

Pari had heard. Probably everyone had heard before Ginger. That was fine. "Watch your back. They'll be coming for you next," she warned Pari.

It felt like she was in a fog as she took her things out of her locker. There wasn't much in it, fortunately. When she finally packed everything, she headed to her car. The security guards at the hospital's front door glared at her.

She made it to her car and dumped her things into the trunk. Then she got inside and sat in the driver's seat for a moment, trying to think and clear her head.

She didn't want to go home. Daehan and Mary were at work, so she picked up her phone and called Autumn.

"They fired me," she said blankly once Autumn picked up.

"What?" her friend asked.

"They fired me."

"Why?"

Ginger told her the story.

"Fuck Pine Health! That shit place constantly racially discriminated against you, excluded you, marginalized you, then fired you? That shithole is full of racists. They don't deserve you!" Ginger could feel Autumn's outrage even through the phone. "I believe in karma. Someday, they'll have to pay for what they've done to you."

Her friend's rage made Ginger feel a bit better. Sometimes, she wondered if she was the crazy one for thinking that people should try to get along and be respectful to each other.

"Thank you," she managed to say after Autumn's diatribe.

Autumn paused, then said, "You know what? Take a break, then apply at AMC, where I work. It's not a perfect place by any means, but try it and see if you like it. Why not?"

"I'll think about it," Ginger said. It made sense, but at the moment, she couldn't figure out where to go at that moment, let alone what she should do after that. She just wanted to escape from her current situation.

Autumn sensed her dear friend's agony through the phone conversation. "Hey, why don't you come over? Let's discuss it more here."

Once Ginger arrived at Autumn's, Autumn offered her some hot chocolate and began talking about her sons in an attempt to distract from her friend's traumatic day.

"I've decided to homeschool Liam and Noah. Noah is on a couple of medications now. His neurologist put him on anti-seizure medication and his psychologist prescribed an anti-anxiety medication. I'm filing suit against the school district, and I've already retained a lawyer. I want to find justice for Noah. I think it will help me heal."

"That makes sense," Ginger replied, almost in a monotone. She felt drained. Everything seemed to have lost feeling, including her legs and her face.

Autumn looked at Ginger carefully and told her, "Now, we need to figure out what will help your situation and get you on the path to healing too."

CHAPTER 17

Seattle, Washington
April 21, 2020

Hyun arrived at work, feeling as if she was on pins and needles. She had discussed the plan for the day with her husband over breakfast. He knew how hard she'd been working to keep Ginger alive, and he wished both of them well as she drove off. This would be a big day, so long as Ginger had done well throughout the night.

When she arrived at the hospital, she found Joe waiting for her at the nurses' station. As soon as he saw her, he smiled and gave her a thumbs up.

Hyun felt relief surge through her as she hurried up to him.

"Got through the night with flying colors," Joe proudly told Hyun as he gazed at Ginger through the window.

"That's a relief," Hyun admitted.

"You've done a great job. This is because of you," he said.

"There were a lot of us involved," she protested.

He looked her in the eyes. "I know how much you've done and what you've had to put up with. Unfortunately, it seems my opinion doesn't matter much."

"It does to me. I appreciate you."

Just then, Dr. Khan walked up to them. "Do you have good news for us?" she asked Joe.

"She came through the night just fine."

Dr. Khan looked over at Ginger as she listened to Joe's report. She seemed pleased and relieved. "Okay, we'll proceed with removing the ECMO line this morning. This afternoon, so long as everything looks good, we'll extubate her. I'll notify the surgeon. Thank you both," she added before she hurried off.

"Good luck," Joe told Hyun with a smile. "I'll see you tonight."

"See you."

Within half an hour, Hyun and Clara were dressed in surgical attire and standing alongside the OR nurse, ready to assist in the removal of the ECMO line by the surgeon at the bedside. Clara administered 25mcg Fentanyl IV for pain control per order. Hyun stood next to the red crash cart and monitored Ginger's condition by constantly shifting her focus from the cardiac monitor to Ginger and back again. The OR nurse assisted in the removal of the ECMO line from Ginger's bilateral groin. The surgeon sutured Ginger's vein and artery back together without any complications.

When the procedure was over, Hyun placed the ECMO machine in the corner of the room and breathed a quiet sigh of relief.

That afternoon, just after lunch, Dr. Khan, Dr. Lim, and Dr. Ortiz huddled around Ginger's bedside, along with Hyun, Clara, and Tom. Dr. Khan wanted a final opinion from the expert before the extubation.

Dr. Ortiz told everyone, "All the numbers are indicating that she is ready for it. Her blood gas looks normal, even her repeat chest X-ray is looking great. I feel confident she'll be fine. Just be diligent during SBT, especially in the first two hours post-extubation. Then we need to closely monitor her for another twenty-four hours."

Dr. Lim added, "I compared today's 12-lead EKG with the ones done in the last few days. All of them showed normal sinus rhythm. Also, her repeat ECHO and her bloodwork have been within the normal limits. I think she is good to go."

"Okay, let's do this," Dr. Khan announced, signaling to Hyun with a nod.

With that, Hyun carefully removed the two-foot-long OG tube out of Ginger's mouth. Hyun quickly discarded the tube into the red biohazard bag, as it was covered with mucus, stomach acid, and bile. All the while, Dr. Khan prepared to remove the endotracheal tube. Tom prepared the Yanker for suction and various oxygen delivery tools, just in case, including the bag valve mask, the non-rebreather mask, nasal cannula, and the oropharyngeal airway.

Carefully, Dr. Khan deflated the cuff after connecting a 20cc syringe at the pilot balloon port in the ET tube, and she removed the tube from Ginger's mouth.

Right after removal of the tube, Ginger coughed, which was expected. Still, her eyes remained closed.

Tom quickly but gently lifted Ginger's head up so she wouldn't aspirate on her own mucus. He suctioned excess mucus from her mouth side to side, placing the Yanker's tip between her gum and cheek. Afterward, Tom put Ginger on the non-rebreather mask to administer ample oxygen that she might need for a short time until she could maintain the appropriate oxygen rate on her own.

During the whole process, Hyun had been staring intently at Ginger, watching for signs that she was starting to respond. Finally, Hyun saw her eyelids flutter and start to open.

"She's awake!" Hyun said ecstatically.

CHAPTER 18

Alderwood, Washington
December 21, 2019

Ginger had been working for Alderwood Medical Center for the past three years as a float RN. She floated through four different departments—ED, PCU, Med/Surg, and ICU.

On this particular Saturday evening, Ginger checked on her patient list when she got to the assigned department at 6:45 p.m. She noticed that Nancy, in room 201 in PCU, was on her list. This would be her eighth time taking care of her, so she knew what to expect.

Nancy had been at the hospital for ten months. The only reason she was there was that none of the nursing homes or home-care facilities would accept her. She was an extremely challenging patient because of her psychological problems. She was bipolar and a master manipulator who loved attracting negative attention.

Nancy had every test run on her that the hospital could possibly run. She had been medically cleared by the entire team of doctors, including cardiologists and neurologists. However, that didn't stop her from faking every possible injury or ailment imaginable. She'd often demanded nurses to feed her even though she was perfectly capable of feeding herself. She would even claim that she couldn't walk and would insist on using a wheelchair, often getting staff to push her around. Yet, if something didn't go her way, she'd been known to get up and run, chasing after nurses who made her angry. Whenever she was bored, she'd fake a heart attack or seizure.

The managers of the different departments would get in screaming matches over who had to take her in because she was "eating up" their budget, so she would be shuttled around from one department to another. She'd been in PCU for almost four months now. Most of the nurses were reluctant to care for her because of how difficult she was. However, none of the nurses were allowed to refuse her. "We all need to take a turn," was what the charge nurse and the manager ordered before each shift. A group of doctors and the nursing team had to develop an individual unique care plan just for her.

At around 8:30 p.m., Ginger gave Nancy her scheduled night pills and made sure that she swallowed all fifteen of her various medications. Nancy, thankfully, did so without giving Ginger any difficulty. She was compliant even when Ginger asked her to lift up her tongue to assess for possible pocketing of the pill.

Afterward, Ginger continued on her rounds. An hour and a half later, Nancy called for her, demanding to be tucked in.

"You're a grown woman. You don't need to be tucked in," Ginger told her firmly, but neutrally. She knew Nancy was just testing the waters and seeing how much she could get away with. "I will stop in and check on you after I complete my round on three other patients."

That seemed to placate the woman for the moment, and Ginger continued on her rounds.

One of her patients in room 202 was experiencing chest pain, so Ginger had to spend extra time with him while giving the doctor an update and then carrying out the orders he gave for care. Ginger saw Nancy standing in the doorway of her room, watching her with a jealous expression on her face.

With the next patient, everything went well without any complications.

When Ginger reached the third patient, she discovered that his blood sugar was 55, which was dangerously low for him. He was close to passing out. She got him some juice and quickly adjusted his medications after letting the doctor know what was going on.

When Ginger finally completed checking in on all three patients, she headed back toward Nancy's room, just as she had promised. She was nearly there when she heard someone shouting, "Lay down! Lay down!"

It sounded like the yelling was coming from Nancy's room. Ginger ran forward and entered the room. She saw Nancy sitting on the edge of her bed with another nurse named Jenna looming over her, shaking her finger at her.

Suddenly, Jenna turned and saw Ginger enter the room. Jenna instantly changed her posture.

"So you're saying you want me to be your nurse instead of Ginger? I'd be glad to!" Jenna said to Nancy in a softer voice. Then Jenna began laughing out loud like they were playing some sort of game.

Jenna made a fierce expression and glared at Nancy. "Put this nitro pill under your tongue!"

"I don't want to!" Nancy refused, shaking her head.

"It's okay," Ginger interceded. "Jenna, can I speak to you in the hall?"

"Not until I'm done with MY patient!" Jenna said, screaming.

Ginger felt outraged over Jenna's sudden invasion of her patient's room, but at the same time, she sensed she needed to take control of the crazy situation. Jenna's manic behavior in front of the patient was like fuel to her already mentally fragile condition.

Ginger made one more effort to remove Jenna out of her patient's room. "Jenna, I've got this. You can go back to your own patients upstairs."

Jenna turned and yelled at her, "She just became MY patient!"

"You cannot administer the nitro on her because she has a history of hypotension, systolic '80s. She doesn't have IV access, and she is not on a cardiac monitor. It is also unsafe to administer nitro without checking her blood pressure. This patient is on a special care plan. I'm familiar with it, and you are not. I know how to care for her. Please leave the room now," Ginger said, keeping her voice as neutral as possible.

"Take the pill and lay down so we can do your EKG," Jenna snarled at Nancy, completely ignoring Ginger.

"Jenna, I told you—"

Jenna whipped around, snarling. She walked up to Ginger and poked her in the chest with her finger. "I AM NOT LEAVING! I AM BEING A PATIENT ADVOCATE!" Jenna screamed at the top of her lungs, her finger jabbing at Ginger with every word.

Ginger stepped outside the room and looked down the hall. She went over to Embler, the charge nurse. She knew that Embler and Jenna were friends, but Ginger hoped Embler could talk some sense into Jenna since she was a charge.

"Embler, would you please assist me? Could you escort Jenna back to the third floor where her patients are?"

Embler stared right past Ginger. She didn't look at her or acknowledge that she was even speaking.

"Embler, I need help with Jenna."

Embler pushed past Ginger and walked down the hall in the opposite direction, never once acknowledging her.

Against her better judgment, Ginger called Daria, the supervisor, to ask for help. Daria was close friends with both Jenna and Embler. If Embler hadn't been willing to do anything, Ginger suspected that Daria wouldn't either. Still, she had to follow protocol and respect the chain of command.

Once she got Daria on the phone, she explained the situation and pleaded for help in getting Jenna out of room 201.

"No, I'm busy. I can't come down right now," Daria said before hanging up.

While Ginger was debating what to do next, Avelino, a new Filipino travel nurse, came downstairs from the third floor. Looking perplexed, he approached Ginger.

"Have you seen Jenna?" he asked. "She's vanished, and she's my preceptor. She's been giving me orientation. I can't pull medication for our patients because I don't have access to Pyxis yet."

"She's here, in this room," Ginger said, leading Avelino to Nancy's room.

Inside, things were even more chaotic as Jenna tried to place nitroglycerin tablets under Nancy's tongue.

Ginger frantically wondered if she'd need to call the police and have Jenna arrested for patient abuse. But first, she had to stop Jenna from administering the medication before it was too late.

"Stop! You can't do that! Jenna, you need to leave this room now!" Ginger firmly commanded.

"No!" Jenna shrieked.

"Please, Jenna," Avelino said, his eyes and voice begging. "I've been looking for you everywhere. I don't have access to Pyxis. I can't pull medication for OUR patients. Some of them are almost an hour overdue at this point. Please come help me!"

"Go wait for me, you stupid Flip!" Jenna screeched.

Avelino jerked as though Jenna had slapped him. He turned and quickly left the room.

"Jenna, your patients are suffering. If you don't leave this room right now, I have to call security and have them escort you back to the third floor," Ginger told her, hoping she was getting through to her.

"You wouldn't dare," Jenna said, laughing again maniacally.

For a moment, Ginger wondered if she should call the psych department instead. Whatever was happening with Jenna, she was causing a scene and endangering both her and Ginger's patients.

"You are leaving me no choice," Ginger called for security.

As she waited for them, she tried to puzzle out why Jenna was even on this floor, let alone interacting with Nancy. Jenna had made it very clear to anyone who would listen that she refused to work with Nancy because of how difficult a patient she was. Her friends in management made an exception by keeping Jenna's name off the RN list for Nancy's care.

Jenna had never once had to care for Nancy, and had no idea if Nancy had an individual care plan. Plus, protocol dictated that you always checked in with a patient's primary nurse before doing anything with them. This whole thing made no sense.

A few minutes later, Ginger heard a few sets of footsteps approaching Nancy's room.

"They're here," Ginger said to Jenna.

Jenna poked her head into the hallway.

"I'll leave you bitches to yourselves," Jenna snarled. She threw Nancy's medication on the floor and then walked slowly, almost regally, out of the room. Once she was outside, she pressed back up against the wall to the room, still refusing to leave the floor.

"I'm out of the room, but I refuse to leave this patient," Jenna informed the guards.

"Can you please escort her to the third floor where her own patients are waiting?" Ginger asked them.

The security guards stood there, looking unsure of what to do. Ginger had a sudden, sickening feeling that even though she was the one who had called them and they could verify that Jenna wasn't on the appropriate floor, they'd side with her. Jenna and both security guards were white.

Just then, Avelino returned. It was obvious he was in distress—whether it was from the frustration of not being able to help his patients or from the ethnic slur Jenna had hurled at him, or a combination of both.

"Please, Jenna," Avelino said, his face covered in sweat. "I'm begging you. Come back to the third floor with me and help me get the medication for the patients. They're screaming in pain, and I can't access Pyxis without you. I need to administer the IV pain medication. Everyone upstairs I've asked for help just tells me you have to do it since you're my preceptor."

Jenna rolled her eyes. "Anyone ever tell you what a whiny bastard you are?" she snapped at him.

Ginger wanted to say something, but Nancy began screaming in the room, so she turned and went in to deal with her.

"Are you okay?" Ginger asked Nancy.

Nancy was visibly upset. Ginger couldn't blame her for that.

"I want to be taken to the Emergency Department," Nancy insisted.

"I'll get someone to wheel you over," Ginger said.

She stepped out of the room hesitantly. She felt relief flood through her when she didn't see Jenna or Avelino in the hallway. Hopefully, that meant they were upstairs attending to their patients. The security guards had also left.

She found Embler and informed her that Nancy had requested to be wheeled over to ED.

"I'll get Dan to take her," Embler said curtly, without even looking at Ginger.

At least this time she acknowledged I was speaking, Ginger thought with relief.

"Dan! Take 201 down to the ED," Embler shouted across the floor.

Dan, a middle-aged, tall African-American man who had always been pleasant to Ginger, waved to Embler in acknowledgement.

A minute later, Ginger met Dan at the nurses' station. He stopped with an empty wheelchair on his way to Nancy's room. He then leaned forward and lowered his voice.

"That was messed up," he said.

"You saw that?" Ginger asked.

"Saw it. Heard it. Who could help it?" he asked. "Look, I've been a CNA for over twenty years. I've never seen such disrespect, bullying, and unprofessional behavior in my entire career. Jenna is awful, and she always treats me like dirt. I always figured maybe she had a problem with Black people or maybe she felt superior since she's an RN and I'm just a CNA. Now I know. She is mentally ill and a hardcore racist. She needs to be fired and have her license revoked. I'll be happy to write you a full report."

"I'm glad at least one person supports me," Ginger said to him gratefully. "Thank you, I appreciate it. By the way, how did Jenna even end up on this floor?"

"I think I can help out there. I saw Nancy wheeling herself toward the elevator and then coming back with Jenna a few minutes later. I think Nancy was doing her usual job of stirring up trouble."

"But why would Jenna come with her? Jenna has never wanted to care for her. Jenna doesn't even…" She stopped talking, telling herself to hold her tongue.

"Care for the patients she has?" Dan asked. "I know. She neglects her patients all the time and never does her mandatory rounds. She just makes up fake reports. Of course, it's easy because she has a connection with the leadership team. She also manages to throw temper tantrums so she only ends up with the easy patients."

Ginger nodded. It was refreshing to talk to a coworker who saw things clearly and wasn't afraid to tell the truth.

"You know what's so evil about her, on top of everything else? She despises nurses who are confident and work hard. She's probably wanted to screw you for a long time because you are the complete opposite of who she is as a nurse. She saw an opportunity tonight and took it. You get that, right? I'm sure Nancy faked chest pains or something, but ultimately, this was about Jenna having a chance to throw shade at you. It's okay though. I'll report what I saw."

Ginger heaved a sigh of relief. "Thank you for your support. And I'm sorry that she's been awful to you too."

"Don't sweat it. I just never thought I'd live to see someone act like that in a hospital who wasn't bound for the psych ward."

Dan then placed Nancy in the wheelchair, and he wheeled her down the hall on their way to the ED. All the craziness had put Ginger behind schedule, and she scrambled to get to her next patients.

When she was done with the rest of them, about half an hour later, she learned that the ED had medically cleared Nancy and was going to be discharging her shortly. The ED charge nurse informed Ginger, "She won't go back to your floor, nor will she need to be re-admitted to the hospital. Our social worker has found a place for her."

When Ginger's twelve-hour night shift was finally over, she was able to confirm that Nancy had indeed been discharged. Ginger wanted to discuss Jenna's incident with her manager, Joanna, in person, but she couldn't since it was Sunday morning. So she wrote an email to Joanna instead, describing the incident in detail and included Dan's name as a witness. She cc'd Jenna's managers, Kathy and Marie, in the report.

Ginger was still tired when she arrived at work on Monday evening, two days after the incident. She hadn't slept well, thinking about everything that had happened. She figured she'd hear back soon from Joanna. She wondered if Kathy and Marie would also chime in.

When she reached the nurses' station, one of the nurses, Emma, had an odd look on her face.

"What's going on?" Ginger asked.

"I don't know, but Kathy has asked anyone who can do so to head to the breakroom for a minute."

Ginger's shift didn't start for another fifteen minutes, so she walked with Emma to the breakroom. When they reached it, the first thing Ginger noticed was a cake on one of the tables.

"Is it someone's birthday?" she muttered to Emma.

"Not that I know of," Emma said, frowning.

There were about a dozen nurses and other staff members present. Kathy and Marie were standing together, and Kathy raised her hands to silence the room.

"We're here to celebrate a nurse who has demonstrated the highest standards of care and compassion," she announced.

Ginger glanced around, wondering who was being honored. It sounded like the managers were giving out a Daisy Award to someone. The Daisy Award was given to a nurse who provided extraordinarily compassionate care to his or her patients and families every day.

"It is our honor and privilege to give this Daisy award to Jenna. She provided exceptional care to Miss Nancy, in room 201," Kathy announced, looking around the crowd.

Ginger stared, flabbergasted. Was this some kind of joke?

Kathy motioned Jenna up. Jenna walked over to stand between Kathy and Marie. She had a smug look on her face that sickened Ginger.

"While taking care of your own four patients and precepting a new nurse, you provided compassionate care to our most difficult patient. Thank you, Jenna, for your selfless care and working tirelessly for our patients. You are an inspiration and an example of what a nurse should be," Kathy gushed.

"You're kidding me," Ginger blurted out.

Fortunately, her outburst was drowned out by the sound of applause as everyone else clapped. Only Emma heard her and stared at her, one eyebrow raised in a silent question.

"And that's not all," Marie piped up. "Jenna, you are also being awarded an all-expense-paid two-week vacation. When you get back, you'll have two months of paid training to work in the ICU. We have a long list of people who want to work in the ICU, but we chose you because you are such an excellent nurse."

"Congratulations on a job well done and on this new step in your career," Kathy chimed in with a huge smile.

"There has to be a mistake. They must not have seen my report yet," Ginger mumbled to herself.

"What is it?" Emma asked Ginger.

"That's not what happened at all," Ginger said. She hurried forward, wanting to let Kathy and Marie know what had happened.

She reached Kathy. Before she could say anything, Kathy turned and gave her a cold stare.

"You," Kathy said, practically spitting the word, "are to report to the CNO's office."

Sheila was the Chief Nursing Officer. Ginger wondered why Kathy would deliver Sheila's message, especially after having such a phony ceremony for Jenna.

Kathy turned away sharply, clearly dismissing Ginger.

Ginger didn't know what was going on, but she headed straight for Sheila's office. Once there, she was quickly escorted inside, and she found Sheila and Joanna, her manager, waiting for her. Neither woman looked happy. Sitting in the corner was Josie, union representative and one of the charge nurses in PCU.

"Close the door!" Sheila barked at Ginger.

She complied quickly, then Sheila lurched to her feet and began yelling at Ginger, "You think it's a good idea to call a security guard on your co-worker? A good nurse knows how to communicate with their co-workers! You must talk to her face to face. You should never call a security guard on your co-worker, never. We are going to send you to a special training called the Art of Communication!"

She snatched up a piece of paper off her desk and thrust it at Ginger. "Call this number and pick a date!"

Ginger was stunned and humiliated. How was it that Jenna was being celebrated and promoted for what she'd done, and Ginger was being forced into communication training?

She looked at Joanna, but her boss just shook her head. "I'm ashamed that one of my nurses acted so badly," she said regretfully.

"I'm not the one who acted badly," Ginger protested.

"Of course you are. It is wrong to call security on your co-worker. Isn't that right, Josie?" Sheila coaxed.

Josie was staring down at the floor, refusing to look up at any of them. "Yes," she answered, her voice barely audible.

In a flash, Ginger understood. Because of her chronic back pain that was unfixable, even with surgery, Josie was unable to provide direct patient care. She needed to keep her charge position, so if she spoke her mind and supported Ginger, she could lose the position and, ultimately, her job. She was as much under management's thumb as Ginger was.

"Dan will tell you what happened," Ginger said, struggling to keep her voice steady. "He said he'd provide you a letter about what happened that night."

"Upon serious reflection, Dan has declined to discuss the incident further," Joanna said with a smirk.

They were able to scare him into being quiet too. Bile rose in the back of her throat. Ginger felt deep disgust and betrayal. How did they expect her to work under these conditions?

Ginger managed to nod, grab the paper, and leave the room.

She was halfway to the hospital cafeteria when Josie caught up with her.

"I'm sorry," Josie whimpered softly.

"I can take it to the union leadership. I don't have to involve you," Ginger said.

"No, you can't," Josie whined.

"Why not?" Ginger demanded, turning to look at her.

"You'll never win. It's your word against theirs, and you're…"

"I'm what?" Ginger asked.

Josie averted her eyes. "You know."

"I'm what?" Ginger demanded.

"You're not like Sheila, Joanna, Kathy, and Marie."

"You mean I'm not dishonest? I'm not a liar? I'm not someone who cares more about profit than patients? What is it I'm not, Josie?"

"Don't make me say it," Josie pleaded.

"Well, you're going to have to because I don't know what makes me different."

Josie stood, fidgeting from one foot to another, her aching back clearly hurting her even more under stress.

"Just say it," Ginger said.

"You're not…white."

There it was. The silent specter that dogged Ginger's every step. She had hoped so badly that things would be different here. She'd tried so hard to pretend that she imagined all the slights, manipulation, and disparaging comments.

"No, I'm not," she said. "And that's a problem?"

"For some," Josie admitted, still unable to look her in the eye.

"And Jenna is white," Ginger noted.

"You're both represented by the union. They'd have to pick sides. And Jenna has management on her side."

"And she's white," Ginger repeated.

"Yeah," Josie said. "I'm sorry."

It had been two weeks since the incident. Ginger had already started her special communication training, and every second she spent in that classroom felt like an insult to her intelligence.

She made it home, feeling exhausted and unappreciated. She checked her mail and found a letter from the Washington State Department of Health. As she held the letter in her hand, she felt a momentary glimmer of hope. She had reported Jenna's unprofessional and negligent behavior in detail to the department.

The envelope contained a single piece of paper with only one paragraph. Her eyes went right to the pertinent part:

"We didn't find any negligent action on the part of the nurse in question. We are hereby withdrawing your complaint."

Ginger let out a long, painful sigh. How was it that Jenna was going to get away with what she'd done? It was monstrous.

Ginger grabbed a pint of ice cream out of the freezer and sat down on the couch. Autumn was at work, so she couldn't call and talk to her. Instead, Ginger started to eat straight from the container as she grabbed her pen and began to write a letter to Eungi.

She paused as she realized that Eungi wouldn't be able to understand the situation. It was entirely out of the norm, unthinkable, and most of all, Eungi had never experienced such an ordeal in her life. Nevertheless, Ginger decided to write a "letter" to Eungi...truly a letter to herself. Letters and diaries gave Ginger a sense of comfort, and in her writing, she was often able to find an answer.

> *Eungi,*
>
> *I feel disgusted. I think this is the final straw. The Department of Health is closing my complaint because they couldn't find anything wrong with Jenna. Such a joke! I wonder if they even bothered to investigate.*
>
> *After doing some research online on a Compensation of Hospital Employees website and on the IRS's website, I've discovered the truth about this place and the rest of the hospitals in the state of Washington. They claim to be a non-profit, but the higher-ups make more than a million a year, plus "bonuses." It's insane how people who don't even see a single patient get paid so much. Yet, I get reprimanded when I can't get enough coverage to take a break and am forced to clock out without having taken it.*
>
> *I obviously want to take my breaks! It's not my fault if I can't.*
>
> *So while the hospital CEOs are raking in millions of dollars, patients die due to lack of care and nurses are forced to work without sufficient breaks. Witnessing this corrupt conduct has*

pushed me right back to square one. The trauma, humiliation, and racial discrimination that I've experienced in the past and in this present hospital have taught me something: I need to stay away from these crazy places. I don't know what to do, but I can't stay here any longer...

The phone rang, interrupting Ginger's train of thought. She noticed that she'd managed to eat half a pint of ice cream as she reached for her phone. She saw it was her mother calling.

"Hi, Mom," she greeted in Korean.

There was a long pause on the other end that made her blood run cold.

"Mom?"

Her mother finally spoke. "Your father had a stroke. He is not doing well."

"I'll get the first flight I can," Ginger said quickly, her heart pounding.

The call disconnected, and the phone slipped from her fingers to the floor.

Seattle, Washington
April 21, 2020

Ginger was dreaming of her parents. It was as though she could hear them and feel them with her. Staying silent, they gave her a hug and gently pushed her forward with a warm smile.

All of a sudden, she felt like she was suffocating. She could feel her eyes watering, her throat constricting. She could feel...

She could feel pain in her throat. That was her first sensation. Slowly, she became aware of other things. There was sound, then there was light. At first, it was muffled, but she finally realized she was hearing voices and the beep of machinery that sounded very familiar to her.

I'm in the hospital, she realized. Of course she was. She had collapsed. She remembered that.

The voices slowly became clearer, and she could make out words. There seemed to be several voices speaking at once.

"She's awake!"

She opened her eyes slowly. She saw several people surrounding her. She could easily tell they were all medical staff by looking at their partial PPE and an eye shield. She realized she didn't know any of them.

A doctor was quick to speak up. "Miss Kim, you're at the hospital. We just extubated you. Can you wiggle your fingers if you hear us?"

Ginger blinked rapidly, opening her eyes wider as she attempted to move her fingers.

"Good! Excellent!"

"Oxygen 97 percent. Switching her to a plain nasal cannula and three liters oxygen," a male RT said as he worked.

"Miss Kim, I'm Doctor Khan. You've been out for the past five weeks. I've been your primary doctor for the entirety of that time."

Ginger blinked in surprise. Five weeks was a long time.

"Today is April 21st, 2020. You became very ill from COVID-19. We almost lost you several times."

"Really?" Ginger asked, her throat hoarse and painful. "By the way, you can call me Ginger."

"Yes, you made it through!"

But the smile slowly left Dr. Khan's face, and Ginger instinctively realized there was bad news coming.

Dr. Khan cleared her throat. "Ginger, I do need to tell you something. You suffered from many COVID-19 related complications. You had terrible blood clots in both your legs."

Ginger looked down and cried out as she saw what was left of her legs. She moaned as tears began streaming down her cheeks. Hyun quickly stepped forward and offered her tissues.

So many thoughts rushed through Ginger's mind. She wondered if they'd done everything they could to prevent the amputation. She worried about what the future was going to hold since she was now disabled. She thought of her brother and how hard this must be on him, knowing that he would have been the one to approve the procedure. She couldn't even begin to wrap her mind around what it was going to be like to learn how to live like this.

She would, though. She'd worked with patients who had lost their legs. She'd seen them go through physical therapy to learn how to cope and gain whatever control over their bodies and lives they could. If they could do it, so could she.

The important thing was that she was alive. She was grateful for that even as she realized she needed time to process and grieve.

"I can still feel my feet," she said.

"As you are already aware, that is Phantom Limb Syndrome," Dr. Khan said.

Ginger nodded, knowing what it was. At least, she knew about it in a clinical sense, but experiencing it herself was an entirely different thing.

"This is your nursing staff who've been taking care of you," Dr. Khan said.

"I'm Clara," the older woman said.

"I'm Hyun," the other nurse told her. "I've been managing your ECMO. You are a true miracle. I'm so glad you pulled it off, as not many people made it through. This virus has been very cruel. I am happy to finally be able to say hello."

"Hello, and thank you both," Ginger responded with a weary smile.

"You have been receiving PT starting on day one after your amputation," Dr. Khan said. "I'm going to put you on home PT and OT for several months. You still have your IJ line on the right side of your neck. We'll remove it as soon as you can pass the PO challenge, but for now, you get ice chips."

Ginger nodded in understanding. "I'm not hungry anyway," she assured the doctor.

"Good. I'm going to check back with you in a little while. For now, I know your brother and sister-in-law would like to hear from you."

"Are they here?" Ginger asked, eyes filling with tears.

"No, because no visitors are permitted in any hospital right now," Dr. Khan said gently. "But we'll get them on a video call for you in just a minute."

"Thank you," Ginger said, feeling an intense surge of emotion.

There was a flurry of activity for a minute, then Clara called Daehan and Mary. Ginger didn't know why, but she felt nervous as she waited for them to answer.

When the video flicked on, and she could see her brother and sister-in-law, Ginger croaked out "hello" before starting to cry.

"Hello! Hello!" both Daehan and Mary kept saying over and over as they beamed and wept.

"Hi," Ginger said.

"We're so glad you're okay," Mary said, because Daehan was crying too hard to speak. She was crying too, but she was also smiling so widely it made Ginger's cheeks ache to look at her.

"We love you so much, little sis," Daehan finally said, struggling to get the words out. Mary nodded fiercely up and down.

"I love you both," Ginger echoed.

Daehan and Mary spoke, catching her up on everything in the past weeks. It turned out that most of what they had to talk about was what had happened to her. They told her that Autumn and the twins were doing all right, as of a couple days earlier. Ginger was relieved to hear that. She couldn't imagine what would happen if Autumn had caught the virus at work and spread it to her boys without realizing it.

"Okay, you should probably let her rest now," Clara said, breaking into the conversation without asking Ginger for permission to end to the call. "We'll call again tomorrow."

Clara unceremoniously hung up the video call. Ginger just stared at Clara, then at the empty screen. Ginger didn't want to say anything, not wanting to ruin the celebratory day by fighting with one of her nurses, but tomorrow seemed like such a long time to wait for more contact with her loved ones.

She suddenly thought of all those people she'd watched die alone in a hospital without any loved ones at their bedside. Her heart broke as she realized that now so many people were dying alone in hospitals.

It was all too much to bear. She closed her eyes and leaned her head back, trying not to let the weight of the world and her own upended life crush her to pieces.

She listened as Clara told Hyun, "The patient fell asleep. I'm gonna go outside and get some fresh air."

Reflexively, Ginger opened her eyes and looked at Clara, then closed them again. She knew what that meant, as she had heard it so many times before from other co-workers—to go outside to smoke a cigarette.

"You go on, I'll take my break after you return," she heard Hyun reply.

She heard footsteps leaving the room, then felt a light pressure on her shoulder. Ginger opened her eyes and looked into Hyun's compassionate gaze.

"I'm so sorry. I know it's a lot to take in," Hyun said gently.

Ginger looked up at her. "Thank you for understanding."

There was something about Hyun's voice that seemed familiar to Ginger.

"It really is a miracle that you're alive, even if it doesn't feel that way to you right now," Hyun added.

Ginger nodded.

"I'll come back later, and we can sit and talk for a while if you're up to it. We can call Daehan and Mary again if you like."

Ginger met Hyun's eyes again. She couldn't believe it. "How did you know? You read my mind. I really appreciate it." Ginger smiled and happily dropped one of the ice chips in her mouth.

Hyun smiled at her. "I know they'd like that too. They're very sweet people, and they love you very much." She stood up. "I'll see you in a couple of hours. If you need anything, press the button and I'll get here as soon as I can."

Ginger felt a kind of peace settle over her. She closed her eyes and tried to rest.

Kirkland, Washington
January 30, 2020

The day Ginger arrived home in South Korea, her father died. He would have been 100 years old in May.

The next day, Daehan and Mary arrived, too late to say goodbye to him.

Two weeks after their father's passing, their mother also suddenly died, shocking all three of them.

Daehan and Ginger stayed in their childhood home for several weeks and visited their parents' graves every day. They did so out of respect toward their parents and as part of their own grieving ritual. Eungi cooked for them every day, saying it was the least she could do.

When it was time for them to get back to the U.S., they donated their parents' house and garden to Daehan's college friends, Yusung and Mira, who had since become husband and wife.

Yusung and Mira had a difficult life since the Gwangju massacre. No one wanted to hire a disabled person with a Samchunggyoyukdae background. Mira had become the sole breadwinner for several years until they'd saved enough and rented a small store to fix household electronic equipment. Both worked twelve-hour days, seven days a week, but they hadn't been able to save enough money to purchase their own home.

In light of that, Ginger and Daehan felt good about giving their parents' property to Yusung and Mira. Daehan told them, "It's great to see the house going to a great family. We couldn't be happier. I'm sure our parents will be smiling, looking down at us right now." Daehan and Ginger hoped that Yusung and Mira would live a long and happy life, just as their parents did. In exchange, Yusung and Mira promised to take good care of the property and the graveyard.

The time away had given Ginger space to do a lot of thinking. She'd even sat in her parents' old living room for hours on end, just as she'd done as a child. Now she was retreating from her life to reflect.

She made a decision. Life was too short to continue in the hell she was in. Part of her felt as if she was being chased away by the ugly systemic problems for the third time, like she had when she'd left Alaska and been powerlessly forced out of Pine Health. She needed to get away from the toxic environment she'd been working in. She was no longer able to tolerate the discrimination, xenophobia, exclusion, and disrespect.

To that end, she decided to become a travel nurse and see the world. She rationalized that since it was impossible for her to change things herself, she would wait until the change found her. Until then, traveling from place to place seemed like a good plan. Maybe she would even find a place where she was respected, appreciated for her skills, and embraced for who she was.

She chose Barrow, Alaska as her first destination, where she would be working with the Inupiat people. The nursing director, Aput, had just hired her after their phone interview.

All Ginger wanted was to bury herself under snow and work, keeping the rest of the world at bay. She set about making the arrangements. She was told it might take up to a month to handle all the paperwork. But she could wait, because then she'd be free.

Kirkland, Washington
February 29, 2020

Something was wrong. Reporters on television were talking about a mysterious illness called COVID-19 and announcing that people were dying.

After soaking up as much information as she could, Ginger turned to paper to write down her thoughts. As usual, she addressed her letter to her friend Eungi, even though she was writing down her thoughts for herself.

> *Eungi,*
>
> *It is Saturday, Feb 29th, 2020. Something is wrong in Washington. The reporters are talking about the mysterious illness called COVID-19. People are dying at rapid speed from it. The victims are from Good Care of Kirkland Nursing Facility. All of them are being transferred to Pine Health Hospital since it is right across from the nursing facility.*

About a week after the first death from COVID-19, the news discussed several Pine Health ED staff being infected with COVID-19. They did not give out names. However, some of the Pine Health ED crew who got infected put some updates on social media. They are fearful and anxious.

According to what I've seen on social media, the names of the infected victims are: Dr. Green, Dr. Macintosh, Nicole, Alana, Lorraine, Salena, Adrik, Tony, Sara, George, Lily, Eve, Mia, Nana, Robbi, and Kathy. And the ED managers Gerry, Belle, plus the ED director Fran.

Dr. Macintosh, Gerry, Nana, Fran, George, Lily, Adrik, Alana, Salena, Tony, Chase, and Nicole were transferred to the higher-level hospital due to the severity of their illness.

I don't know what's going on, but I have a feeling the sooner I get out of AMC and Washington, the better. I get to turn in my resignation this coming week. In just a couple of weeks, I'll be writing to you from Alaska again! It would be great if you could all come visit.

Ginger

Alderwood, Washington
March 5, 2020

"What the hell is this?"

Ginger was in the office of her new manager, Jaeger. When she had returned from overseas, she discovered that Joanna had moved to a different position. Jaeger was tough, a former military man who enjoyed reminding people of that fact. He was glaring at her now as if she was an insubordinate recruit.

He crumpled up a piece of paper and threw it at her. It bounced off her chest and fell to the floor. Ginger froze.

Jaeger growled at her, "This is garbage now! You can't leave!"

Ginger had left her resignation letter in Jaeger's mailbox the day before. Apparently, he'd finally gotten around to reading it.

Ginger tried to find her voice. "I'm leaving for Alaska."

"Oh, no, you're not," he said, clearly angry. "You can't quit during the COVID pandemic. If you do, I'll make sure that you don't get your job in Alaska or any other jobs that you might apply to in the future."

"You can't force me to stay," Ginger said, beginning to shake.

"Look, you only need to stay until this COVID thing settles down or I get more nurses. We're talking only a few months, say, until May. After that, I'll let you go free. Hell, I'll even give you excellent references for your future employers. Think about it," Jaeger said in a way that implied there was nothing for her to think about.

He smirked at her, then said, "Get back to work."

Ginger felt despair as she left his office. Reporting Jaeger's hostile and threatening behavior to HR or the nurses' union was out of the question. No one would believe or support her, so she felt there was no choice but to stay. *Only until May*, she told herself.

She wasn't sure if Jaeger could really make good on his threats, but she wasn't in a position where she had the luxury to find out. If she could just stick it out for a couple of months, she would be free from an evil manager forever.

For once though, Ginger wasn't alone in her dislike of a manager. None of the nurses or CNAs liked Jaeger. He would show up extra early, at 5 a.m., in his long burgundy leather coat with shiny black leather boots that reached to his knees, to intimidate his staff. He would also stand in the hallway between the patients' rooms and the nurses' station, right in the most high-traffic area, and glare to the right and to the left.

Ginger hadn't ever seen such threatening behavior displayed so openly in her entire career. He was six-foot-three, and his mannerisms, coupled with his long trench coat, made him resemble a Gestapo agent. Dealing with him gave Ginger flashbacks to her childhood in Gwangju during the massacre.

Once Jaeger assumed command of the medical floor and the float department, he immediately set out to increase the financial earnings from his two departments. Each month, he managed to make the hospital a large profit by manipulating, bullying, and intimidating his nurses and CNAs. Jaeger would agree with nurses and CNAs to supply more staff whenever there was a sudden increase in the number of patients in the two departments he managed. However, he would just as quickly turn around and issue orders *not* to provide extra nurses and CNAs. After all, more patients with the same staff meant an increase in department profit. He made no secret of his desire to one day run the entire hospital, and he thought this was his ticket to the top.

His policies made things a living hell for the staff. If the department was swamped, and a nurse or CNA had to end up clocking out for the day without taking a break, they would get hauled into his office and be rigorously grilled about why they didn't take it. Ginger herself had been forced to give a similar account once already. She had told him she couldn't take a break since she had to care for six patients without any CNA's assistance during an entire twelve-hour shift. Two of those patients had been high acuity, which required twice the effort and time spent on nursing care than the rest of the patients in that assigned department. She had notified the charge nurse and asked for help, but never received assistance from a CNA.

Jaeger managed to blame Ginger, even though she'd report the problem about taking the break to the charge nurse ahead of time. He warned Ginger against repeating that behavior, telling her, "Nurses who don't take their break are incompetent. I hope we don't have to have a meeting like this again. If you need to clock out as 'no break', you must notify your charge nurse, send me an email, and explain the reason why."

He also went after nurses who clocked out even a single minute late. Sometimes, it was inevitable for a nurse to clock out late if a patient became ill around the shift change. Nurses and CNAs would have to stay late in order to chart the care that they provided to their patients. Jaeger wanted people to clock out on time and then stay late to do their charting—without pay. Ginger had reported this to the union, but it had gone nowhere, so she hadn't bothered to follow up.

No one wanted to speak up against him. *No one wants to stand up*, Ginger thought bitterly. She no longer wanted to either. Not only had she been burned before, but she also believed that his retaliation would be disastrous for her future career opportunities.

Things were only getting worse now that every department in the hospital was packed with coronavirus patients and corona rule-out patients. They'd even had to temporarily close both the surgical and mother-and-baby units to convert them to COVID units, in order to accommodate the mounting number of virus-related patients.

When Ginger came in for her shift the next day, she discovered several nurses milling about, complaining about the new protocol.

"What's going on?" Ginger asked one of them.

"No masks, no face shields, and no eye shields."

"What?" Ginger asked, startled.

The nurse glanced over Ginger's shoulder, her jaw tightening. "You'll see," she said before hurrying off.

Ginger turned and saw Jaeger approaching. "Okay, gather around everyone!" he said in a booming voice that stopped all conversation. Ginger reluctantly approached the nurses' station with the others who were coming on shift.

"No strict PPE is required in caring for the corona patients," he began.

With that, the nurses and CNAs around her started muttering.

"Shut up and listen! The N95 masks, face shields, and the eye shields are not to be used."

"We need to protect ourselves," one of the male nurses spoke up.

"Don't be a moron," Jaeger snapped. "You don't need any masks or shields here on the medical floor when you take care of COVID patients or COVID rule-out patients. But if your patient has a coughing fit, then you may wear a surgical mask! Also, do not wear a mask around the hallway. If I catch anyone breaking these rules, there'll be hell to pay. Now get to work!"

Jaeger stalked off. The male nurse who had spoken up stood there, looking ashen. "That maniac is trying to kill us all," he whispered.

CHAPTER 19

Seattle, Washington
April 24, 2020

It was three days after Ginger's extubation. She was recovering well. An ultrasound of her upper legs and stumps were free of any blood clots. All her blood tests, an X-ray of her lungs, and a repeat ECHO to her heart were normal. She'd been told she might not even need to have another blood gas check unless she crashed again.

It had been incredibly painful when the nurses or RTs collected blood from her arterial vessel, which gave her an even deeper sympathy for every patient for whom she'd had to check blood gas.

Yet, her recovery was going smoothly and she felt so much better than she had the day before. She remembered how sick she'd been when she'd called the ambulance, struggling to breathe. She was incredibly grateful for her medical team at the hospital, particularly Hyun, who, true to her word, had stopped by two more times to help her with video calls to Daehan and Mary.

On one of those calls, she had found out that Autumn had also been infected. Autumn was now in the ICU, only a couple of rooms away from Ginger. Fortunately, Autumn had called Daehan and Mary right before she called the ambulance for herself. Daehan and Mary had gone over, picked up Liam and Noah, and taken them to their house, where they'd been staying ever since. Thankfully, none of them contracted the disease. It sounded like the boys were doing well despite all the changes.

Ginger was glad the twins had already spent a lot of time with Daehan and Mary. Her brother and his wife often babysat them when Autumn was at work and Ginger couldn't.

There was a light knock on her door, and she looked up to see Hyun standing in the doorway.

"How are you feeling?" Hyun asked.

"So much better, thank you," Ginger said gratefully.

"I checked on your friend, Autumn," Hyun said.

"Thank you. I wish I could see her."

"If you want, I can wheel you by the room so you can wave."

"That would be wonderful," Ginger said, smiling.

"We'll need to get you a gown, gloves, and a mask."

"Whatever it takes."

"Autumn also gave permission for Dr. Khan to go over her treatment plan with you."

"Thank you for all your help," Ginger said.

"No problem," Hyun said with a smile.

Twenty minutes later, wearing a gown, gloves, and mask, Ginger was in the wheelchair. She'd needed Hyun's help to get into it. Sitting in the chair, she felt the loss of her legs anew, and she struggled with the wave of sorrow that crashed over her.

A moment later, the wheelchair was in motion and she pushed her sorrow down. She didn't want to look like she'd been crying or upset when Autumn saw her.

Autumn was in a shared room with five other patients. She had lost so much weight that it shocked Ginger. She looked up and waved through the window as Ginger wildly waved both her hands back at her. Autumn smiled weakly, but then began to cough. After the coughing fit subsided, she looked up again and waved some more.

"Okay, that's enough excitement for now," Hyun said gently.

She wheeled Ginger back to her room. By the time she had gotten back onto the bed again with Hyun's help, Dr. Khan came in.

"I hear you and Autumn are best friends," the doctor said.

"Yes, how is she?" Ginger asked anxiously.

"We're treating her with Remdesivir, dexamethasone, and Tylenol since her case is early-stage compared to yours. Remdesivir shortens recovery time for patients who are not sick enough to be on the vent. Today is day two since the first dose, and I'm hoping she'll be better in a few days. This is based on the forty other patients I've treated with Remdesivir before her. Overall, I feel optimistic about the positive treatment account."

"Thank you, Doctor."

Dr. Khan smiled. "Anything for my star patient," she said warmly.

"I know someone else who wants to see you," Hyun said after the doctor left.

She dialed up Daehan and Mary, who waved excitedly at her.

"Hi," Ginger said, smiling at them.

"How are you?" Mary asked.

"Good. Hyun took me out in the wheelchair and let me wave at Autumn through her window. She's super thin and coughing a lot, but she waved back. The doctor explained to me how she's been treating her."

Daehan nodded. "Since she can't really speak because of the breathing issues and the continuous coughing, we've been communicating through her nurse, Adam. Dr. Khan has been keeping us up to date on her as well since she knows we have her boys with us."

The way Daehan and Mary had risked exposure, along with their lives to take in the boys, proved what she'd known all along—they were both beautiful human beings. The African proverb about it taking a village to raise a child sprang to her mind.

"Every day, we pray for Autumn and you with Liam and Noah," Mary said.

"Thank you," Ginger told her.

They talked for a few more minutes, then it was time to go.

That afternoon, Ginger got her smart phone and went on social media for the first time in six weeks. She posted about how she was doing and could see people immediately responding. She also used it to check on coworkers and acquaintances.

She discovered that at least eleven people she'd known at Pine Health had died from complications related to COVID-19, including Dr. Macintosh, Gerry, Nana, Adrik, Salena, Lily, Alana, Nicole and others. There were more in the ICU, intubated at the same hospital where she was being treated. She thanked God that Pari's name wasn't on either of those lists. It looked like all eleven families of those who had died were suing Pine Health for wrongful death.

She wondered who at AMC might have been infected with COVID besides her.

Alderwood, Washington
March 7, 2020

Ginger had just arrived at work and was getting ready to meet with the nurse coming off shift to get a report on her patients. She was assigned to the PCU again, but this time on the third floor, which neighbored the ICU.

Suddenly, screaming erupted from the ICU across from her. Alarmed, Ginger ran over with several others.

When she got there, she noticed a loose crowd had gathered around Jenna, who was screaming and waving her hands in the air.

"What's going on?" Ginger whispered to one of the ICU nurses.

"Jenna doesn't want to take her turn," the man whispered back.

"Her turn for what?" Ginger asked.

"What do you think?" he said.

Jenna yelled at an African-American nurse, grabbing her. "YOU HAVE TO SWITCH WITH ME!"

"No, I don't!" the nurse told Jenna, batting her hands away and backing away from her.

"I CAN'T BE THE COVID PATIENT'S NURSE! SWITCH PATIENTS WITH ME!" Jenna roared, stalking after other nearby nurses.

Another nurse shook her head in frustration. "We all agreed to take turns with the COVID patients. It's your turn."

Jenna shoved the woman, then turned to a Filipino nurse. She got in the woman's face. "YOU NEED TO SWITCH WITH ME!" she said, voice menacing. Tears were streaking down Jenna's face, and as she kept demanding over and over that the nurse switch with her, the tone of her voice switched from bullying to whining.

When the Filipino nurse managed to break free of her grasp, Jenna started searching the crowd for others. "SOMEBODY ELSE HAS TO TAKE THIS PATIENT!" she screamed.

"There is no one else. The rest of us have already taken care of the COVID patients once or twice before."

"Besides, we're already short-staffed," someone else pointed out.

Jenna shuddered then stood up straight. She stopped crying, wiped her tears, and then glared at everyone.

"I'm sick. I'm going home!" Jenna said, before turning and stomping off.

"She can't do that," several people muttered.

Ginger just shook her head. She wished she could say out loud that she was not surprised by Jenna's antics, but she didn't.

"What are we going to do?" someone asked. "We're already stretched too thin as it is."

Ginger headed back to the PCU. She needed to get ready for her shift. She was halfway there when she heard footsteps running behind her.

"Hold it!" a familiar voice barked.

Ginger turned and saw Jaeger glaring at her. "Where do you think you're going?"

"To PCU to start my shift."

"Change of plans. You'll be in ICU today."

Ginger blinked in shock. "But they need me in PCU."

"They need you in ICU more!" At that moment, Ginger felt pressured to accept the changed assignment. She knew this would quickly turn into a threat, followed by retaliation, if Jaeger didn't get his way. He'd make her life even more hellish and report her to HR for insubordination.

Ginger took a deep breath and said, "I'll be there in five minutes."

"You'd better be," Jaeger growled.

Ginger reported back to the PCU and let them know that she'd been ordered to work in the ICU to cover for Jenna.

"That's unfair and outrageous," one of the nurses said, her face flushing in anger. "We need you here."

Ginger shrugged. "I know, but what can I do?"

"Nothing," the other nurse sighed. "Just be careful."

"You too."

"Yeah, as careful as they'll let us be," the woman said, rolling her eyes. "Can someone tell me how we ended up working in such a chaotic and messed-up environment when we call this country a world-leading developed country? The hospital has plenty of money. They should pony up some of it to buy proper safety equipment."

"I agree," Ginger and another float nurse said in unison.

"You mark my words, something terrible is going to happen because of their negligence, and then they'll be scrambling to cover their asses," the third float nurse warned.

Ginger nodded, but didn't say anything else. There was no point in complaining. She'd learned the hard way over her years in the nursing community that complaining wouldn't change anything. Every time she thought of standing up and drawing a line in the sand, she found it was her against impossible odds. She didn't know how much longer things could continue the way they were, but she had given up thinking that she could change them.

Yet, Ginger understood the float nurse's point very well. She was incredibly nervous working without sufficient personal protection equipment. She knew that nurses and doctors all over the city were contracting the virus, including a number from her previous hospital. As much as she resented some of those people for the way they'd treated her, she would never wish something like this on any of them.

Without the proper safety equipment, they were putting their lives on the line now more than ever before. Yet, they were expected to do it. It was their "duty." They were the front line of a war with a pandemic, and not only did they have no weapons, but they also didn't have protective armor or shields.

Ginger thought her current situation was like what she'd experienced in Gwangju as a child, filled with the chaos and death of innocent people.

She shivered at the terrible, sickening vision that danced in her mind.

It's going to be okay, Ginger tried to reassure herself as she walked back over to the ICU. *You've been doing everything right. You have the N95 mask you were fitted with a year ago, and you've wiped it down after every patient contact. You've been washing your hands constantly and not touching your face.*

She had been seeing COVID-19 patients for the last few days, but it was always nerve-wracking. Several of her coworkers had joked that playing Russian roulette with a loaded gun was safer than seeing a COVID-19 patient.

As soon as she made it into the ICU, she was directed toward a room with a COVID-19 case. She took a deep breath, secured her mask, and headed in.

The patient was Mr. Carter. As a standard part of the nursing assessment and wanting to establish a good patient-nurse relationship, Ginger began by saying hello.

"Hello, Mr. Carter."

He gave no response. He appeared to be either asleep or unconscious. Ginger didn't want to startle him, so she began with a visual assessment. She saw his chest rise and fall, an indication for him breathing. His breathing was slightly labored, even with the oxygen through a nasal cannula- he was using 3 Liters of oxygen. The oxygen rate was 95%. She noted that she'd have to reassess him frequently due to the concerns of his breathing, even with oxygen. She also noted the rest of his vital signs and checked his IV. She noted that there had been no real change from the last time his vitals had been taken.

He stirred slightly and opened his eyes. "Who are you?" he said irritably.

"I'm Ginger. I'm your nurse for this shift," she told him. "Do you know where you are right now?"

"Hospital!"

That was a good enough answer for now. Ginger decided to keep a close eye on him, as his irritability may be a sign of his condition worsening.

"Is there anything I can get for you?" she asked.

"No, just get away from me!"

"Okay. I'll be back to check on you a little later," Ginger said evenly.

She left the room. Some people didn't appreciate having nurses wake them when they'd been sleeping. She was used to that. Frankly, she didn't blame them, but sometimes it couldn't be helped.

She went and washed her hands, then carefully wiped down her mask with a Sani wipe. She let the mask air dry for a minute while she attended to computer charting. It wasn't long enough for it to dry all the way, but she put it on again and headed to the next patient's room.

The night progressed, and things just got busier as more patients were admitted to the ICU. Ginger noticed that all the nurses and doctors looked as tired as she felt. It didn't help when colleagues kept getting sick, or others like Jenna faked it so they wouldn't risk getting exposed to the virus.

At four a.m., Ginger went back to check on Mr. Carter for the fourth time. When she walked into the room, she could tell instantly that his condition had worsened. His breathing was more labored and strained. Even his vitals were unstable with a spiked temperature and an increased heart rate of 120.

She activated the RRT by pressing the yellow button above Mr. Carter's bed. In the meantime, Ginger applied a non-rebreather mask on him for better oxygenation. However, just as she bent over toward Mr. Carter's right arm to connect the Tylenol-filled IV line, he pulled down his mask and spat in her eyes, "Go back to China! It's all your fault!"

Ginger staggered back as the spittle blinded her. She gasped in horror and ran over to the sink in the room. She put her head down and quickly began washing out her eyes. Meanwhile, behind her, Mr. Carter continued to yell obscenities and ethnic slurs.

"What's going on here?" demanded a doctor who had just arrived to respond to the RRT.

"Chinese bitch! Her and her friends created this damn thing!" Mr. Carter roared.

"Ginger, what's wrong?" the doctor asked.

"He spat in my eyes, but the RRT is for his unstable vital signs. His heart rhythm has changed to tachycardia, he is hypotensive, oxygen 80% at 3L, nasal cannula, and he's spiked a fever to 104! He may need to be intubated!" Ginger said hurriedly.

"Let's get you to the eye irrigation station. Can you help her?" the doctor ordered the CNA who appeared next to him. Then the doctor turned and began assessing Mr. Carter.

Ginger was led by one of the ICU CNAs to the eyewash station. She stripped off her mask, which also had spittle on it and was partly wet from her previous eye washing. She dropped the mask on the floor as she bent over and began irrigating her eyes. Shock and horror raced through her.

Will I be okay? Am I going to get COVID from this? How could he blame me for something that has nothing to do with me? I'm not even from China. Even if I was, how can he blame one individual nurse who trying to help him?

But then Ginger remembered the numerous offensive statements and speeches made by the Trump administration, which blamed the Chinese government for the outbreak since the beginning of the pandemic.

Is it really Mr. Carter who should be blamed for spitting on me?

She realized how panicky she was getting. She took a deep breath and told herself, *Come on, Ginger, hold it together. Let's just irrigate your eyes really well.*

It took her about half an hour to finish irrigating her eyes and clean up. She debated briefly on what to do with her mask. Her first instinct was to throw it away in a biohazard container, along with the gloves she'd been wearing. But since she knew she couldn't get another mask, she finally doused it with sanitizer and tried to wash it up as much as possible.

She sat down at one of the computer stations, hands shaking as she filled out the incident report.

"Are you okay?" the nurse at the computer station next to her asked as he slowly moved his chair away from her. There was naked fear in the man's eyes.

"I don't know," Ginger said, her voice trembling.

"Did Mr. Carter really spit on you?" he asked.

"Yes."

"That's murder."

"What?" she said in disbelief and feeling a chill down her spine.

"He knows he has the disease. If he knowingly infected you, that's murder," the man said.

"Only…only if I die," she stammered.

"Yeah."

Looking at him, she could see that he was convinced that could very well happen.

"Maybe it didn't infect me," she said.

"Maybe. You should go home though."

She nodded. Her shift was over in a couple of hours. As soon as she finished filling out the report, she'd talk to the charge nurse about leaving.

The other nurse got up, and she noticed him moving to a different computer farther away. Ginger could feel the fear through her coworkers' behavior around her, which motivated her to go home without delay.

She tried to keep herself calm as she finished filling out the report. Once she was done, she started to stand up, only to find Jaeger towering over her.

"What's this I hear about you going home?" he demanded.

She glanced over and saw that the nurse she had been talking to was nowhere to be seen.

"A COVID-positive patient spit in my face. A lot of it landed in my eyes. I might be infected," she said.

"I don't care if he kissed you on the lips. You're not going anywhere. Not while we're short-staffed."

"But I might be infected, contagious…I think I need to go home."

"And I might be elected president. I don't want your excuses. Now, get your ass in to see your next patient."

"I really think I need to go home."

"You shouldn't be wearing a mask at all! That's what probably scared him!" Jaeger shouted.

"What? What are you saying?"

"All I'm saying is that you need to be more careful. Don't let patients spit on you."

Jaeger was so worked up, he was spitting as he shouted and the veins in his neck protruded. She winced as fine droplets hit her face.

"I don't have to take this," she said, hating that she could hear her voice shaking.

"And I already told you, if you quit on me now, I'll make sure your license isn't worth the paper it's printed on," he said. "Now get off your ass and go see patients."

He turned and started to stalk off, but he paused and turned back as if he'd just remembered something. "And you're working in this department tomorrow and the day after. Apparently, Jenna is going to be home sick for a few days."

As he stormed off, she stared in outrage at his retreat. She wanted to quit. She wanted to report him. Anger threatened to consume her, but it was quickly subsumed by frustration. What good would any of that do? He could utterly destroy her career. He knew it, and so did she.

No one was going to believe a Korean woman over a white man.

Ginger looked at her wet, crumpled N95 mask. It was useless for anything airborne at this point—she was almost certain of it.

Feeling utterly defeated, she discarded it.

Kirkland, Washington
March 10, 2020

Ginger stripped off her clothes and staggered into the shower the minute she got home from work. She was so exhausted. She'd been running crazy shifts and had gone days without a break and sufficient PPE.

When she stepped out of the shower, she knew something was wrong. She felt dizzy and her chest ached. As she struggled to put on her clothes, she realized her breathing was starting to come in short, sharp gasps.

"Oh no," she mumbled as she reached for her phone. She dialed 911. As the operator answered, she gasped out her name and address before falling unconscious to the floor.

CHAPTER 20

Seattle, Washington
April 26, 2020

It was discharge day and Ginger was beyond excited. While they were preparing her paperwork, she was able to call Autumn.

"Hi!" Autumn's voice was still raspy.

"Oh, Autumn! It's so good to hear your voice!" Ginger said, feeling delighted but sad that she was leaving her friend behind at the hospital. "Dr. Khan told me that you're doing better."

"Yes, I can breathe better and I feel so much better. I was hoping they'd send me home today with you, but Dr. Khan says she wants to keep me here a couple more days just to be extra-safe."

"I see. You take care. I'll say hi to your boys and tell them you'll be home soon."

"Thank you. I don't know what I would have done without you and your family," Autumn said gratefully.

"I haven't done anything. It's Daehan and Mary who deserve all the credit."

Just then, Hyun came into the room with a big smile on her face.

"I have to go. They're coming to get me. I'll wave to you as I leave, and I'll call you later tonight," Ginger promised Autumn.

"All ready to get out of here?" Hyun asked cheerfully as Ginger ended the call.

"Am I ever," Ginger admitted. "Honestly, though, I can't thank you enough."

"I was just doing my job," Hyun said humbly.

"And you did it wonderfully. I know it couldn't have been easy."

Hyun nodded, but didn't say anything. She helped Ginger transfer into the wheelchair and made sure she had all her belongings with her. Then they rolled out of the room.

At the nurses' station, there was a small group gathered. Ginger recognized Clara and Dr. Khan as well as several others. When they saw her, everyone burst into cheers and applause.

Ginger was able to take a moment to thank every one of them for the care they'd given her. When they finally continued on, she was able to wave to Autumn, who waved excitedly back at her. She was grateful to see that her friend looked much better than she had just days ago.

Daehan and Mary greeted Ginger at the hospital entrance, wearing their masks and gloves. They exchanged long hugs and wept with joy, while numerous hospital staff continued to cheer Ginger's discharge.

Hyun helped Ginger settle safely in the passenger seat of Daehan's car.

Liam and Noah were waiting inside the car, with their ears covered with headsets. Mary sat behind her husband, next to Noah. Ginger turned and gave each boy a high five.

"Your mom is doing well. She'll be home in a few days," she told them. Ginger was well aware that neither Liam nor Noah understood what "a few days" meant since neither of them really grasped the concept of time. So she explained it to them by pantomiming sleeping through numerous gestures. "You sleep, and sleep, and when you wake up, you'll see your mom."

"These are from Ginger," Mary said to the boys as she handed them each a yellow Lego bucket that Ginger had asked Mary to order online for them.

Both boys took their buckets and stared at them. Instead of "thank you," Liam responded by saying, "I love rainbow, red and orange, yellow and green, pulpo and blue", which was a typical response for autistic individuals. Noah made funny faces.

"You guys are good kids. I love the rainbow too. I like your funny faces," Ginger said tenderly, so grateful to see them safe.

Kirkland, Washington
May 18, 2020

It was the fortieth anniversary of the Gwangju Democratization Movement. Since Korea was a day ahead, Daehan and Mary watched the anniversary ceremony online the day prior.

They had video-called Ginger mid-morning that day. Daehan had been overwhelmed with emotion and pain. The anniversary felt so real for him, especially after hearing multiple former comrades give testimonial speeches through a massive video chat that included Yusung and Mira. He remembered everything clearly as if the beating, the chopping off of his fingers while being tortured, and starvation in Samchunggyoyukdae had happened yesterday. He spoke of the endless retaliation that had pushed him out of the country when Jun became the president of South Korea.

But he had brightened at the end of the call, saying that if it hadn't been for those circumstances, he wouldn't have met Mary, which made Mary glow with happiness. Ginger told them both how happy she was that they were all family.

Once she hung up with them, Ginger faced the day ahead. Her physical therapist would be coming by to assist her. Ginger was hoping to be fitted for prosthetic legs in two weeks, so they were doing what they could for now so she'd be ready for them.

Every day, she voraciously soaked up news about the virus and scoured social media for word about acquaintances and coworkers. Today, though, she just wasn't in the mood. Her mind was rooted firmly in the past, thinking about her brother, their parents, her friends, and everyone who had made sacrifices for democracy, for freedom.

Freedom was a funny thing. She had always thought of America as the land of freedom. Ultimately, it was a land of oppression, just like other countries, but that oppression was more hidden than most. The discrimination she and her fellow non-white nurses had experienced was appalling. The discrimination Autumn's children faced was monstrous.

For nearly two decades, she had been helpless to do anything about it. Every time she'd had an opportunity to take a real stand, she hadn't, afraid of what it would do to her career. Well, regardless of how her prosthetic legs worked out, her bedside nursing career was over. It was time to rethink her life. The more she did so, the more she found herself thinking of her beginnings.

When she was a child, she had hidden, huddled alone and frightened, in her parents' living room. In many ways, she had never left that living room. She certainly hadn't left the feeling of being huddled alone, frightened, worried that someone was going to hurt her for no good reason. It was time for that to change. America, for all its shortcomings, was a place where reinventing oneself was not unheard of. It was time for her to do just that.

The more she thought, the more an idea began to form. She started doing some research, and her idea began to really take shape. She realized that all her life, she had felt that she owed something to her brother and the others who had fought, with many losing their lives. Now, she knew that she owed them more than she had thought, but in a different way.

Kirkland & Alderwood, Washington
June 16, 2020

Two weeks passed quickly after the fitting. There suddenly seemed so much to do, and Ginger was busy researching how to put her plan into motion.

The day she had been fitted for her prosthetic legs was a freeing one. There was something revelatory about the whole experience, and her physical therapist was delighted when Ginger took a few steps on her own with her new legs.

Around 5:30 p.m., Daehan and Mary dropped dinner off at Ginger's house and Autumn's. The three households linked up and shared their meal together on a video call.

All three households placed their Miyeok-guk, Bulgalbe, steamed rice, and Kimchee on the table in front of them. It was the same delicious dishes that Ginger and Daehan's mother had fixed when he and his friends were released from the Samchunggyoyukdae.

Daehan proposed a toast to Ginger and Autumn, "I want to congratulate you both. To your health and happiness!"

It had been a long time since Ginger had eaten all four dishes, and somehow, this time seemed the most special. The flavors of the food were exquisite. Now Ginger understood how her dear brother must have felt when he tasted their mother's special dishes that day. Ginger tasted each dish by remembering her parents, and the day of Daehan and his friends' release from the camp. In a way, Ginger felt as though she was at the same place where Daehan and his friends once were—celebrating a new beginning. She also remembered her father's endless tears that he'd shed over her brother while preparing Daehan's bath.

Ginger wanted to believe her parents would not cry over her legs. Instead, she tried to imagine that if they were still living, they would cheer her on and encourage her to live her life to the fullest, given her second chance in life.

In that moment, Ginger felt as though her parents were with her, which made her feel safe and allowed her to believe everything would be okay.

"I could eat this three times a day!" Ginger said cheerfully.

"This is so delicious, it makes me cry. Thank you so much," Autumn said. "Look, even Noah and Liam are cleaning their plates."

Daehan told everyone he had an announcement. "So we both officially gave our notice. We are retiring."

"Congratulations!" Autumn said.

Ginger congratulated them as well. She was pleased for them both. She knew they had many sleepless nights due to Daehan's stress at work.

"So what are you going to do with all that leisure time?" Autumn asked.

Daehan and Mary exchanged a look. Then Daehan cleared his throat. "Well, we've decided to volunteer our time in the organization where concerned individuals are trying to recognize and honor people who fought against Jun's Martial Law and brutality during the 5.18 Democratization Movement."

Ginger wasn't surprised by his words. She'd had a feeling they might do something like that, just from the little hints they'd been dropping the last couple of weeks.

Daehan was still her hero. All along, he'd never lost sight of who he was.

"I'm not surprised," Ginger said. "But please be careful. Jun jailed Priest Jo and framed him for treason because he volunteered to help the victims of Gwangju Democratization activists. Jun even called him a liar when he stood against him in the trial to give a statement on Gwangju's helicopter massacre. After forty years, Jun still lives like a king in South Korea. He has never been charged for what he's done. That says something about how influential he still is in Korea."

"Yes, please be careful. The three of us will miss you guys," Autumn chimed in.

"Hey, we're not leaving forever. We'll come back for visits from time to time," Daehan said.

"You've got to do what your heart desires. I'm going to miss you both," Ginger said.

"We still have some time yet, since we have to sell our house and wait for the COVID vaccine," Mary said, looking fondly at Daehan.

Her brother smiled back, then dropped his eyes and changed his voice to a more serious tone. "What about you, sis? Have you figured out what you want to do now?"

Ginger could tell he was hesitant to ask about her future. But she was more than ready to tell all of them what she had been working on and thinking about for the last few weeks.

"Well, ever since I was fitted into the prosthetic legs two weeks ago, I've been practicing walking and I'm getting better at it every day."

Everyone burst into applause and congratulated her. Ginger smiled and nodded.

"What was strange was that I found a new kind of peace when I was standing on my prosthetic legs. I finally felt like I no longer owed a debt to the 606 people who died during the Gwangju massacre. I'd always thought I owed my life to them. I couldn't help but think that their sacrifice made my existence possible. Finally, today, I feel that burden lifted off my shoulders. It may sound weird, but I feel like I paid off my debt with my legs."

Daehan was visibly moved by her words. But before he could comment, Ginger continued, "Obviously, I'm no longer able to take the travel assignment in Barrow, Alaska and I'm unable to do bedside nursing care. However, I'm not going to sue anyone. Instead, I'm going to focus on healing and moving forward. Besides, I now realize that I battled against an army of entitled Caucasian co-workers during my eighteen years of employment within U.S. hospitals. I innocently believed that all hospitals support and listen to each employee's concerns and complaints about discrimination. I realize now that the hospital's discrimination-reporting websites only exist for the formality, not for real improvement.

"It didn't matter if I provided excellent care to the patients or if I worked twice as hard and efficiently as the Caucasian nurses. They weren't going to allow me to advance in my career or recognize my work, even when I worked so hard to save patients' lives. They expected me to be submissive and accept discrimination. I feel like I've been forced to eat my white co-workers' leftovers—I was invited for dinner at their house, but was only allowed to sit on the floor and eat the food that others dropped. Even if I had recovered without my amputation and was physically fit to return to bedside nursing, I probably would choose not to. I realize now that I need to take a different path."

Ginger took a deep breath. "I want to help change systemic racism, so others won't go through what I've gone through. I'm working on a website for Asian, Hispanic, and African-American medical professionals to discuss work-related racism online. The public must be educated about the negative outcome when patients or their family members attack and racially discriminate against their medical professionals. I also plan to work to change the tax code, so that hospitals and religious organizations are viewed as what they truly are: for-profit organizations. I'll be collecting signatures to promote this movement online. I'm also going to lobby to levy higher taxes on all top-paid corporate CEOs, business leaders, business owners, and politicians. I'm looking for volunteers who have similar beliefs as mine. I need to team up with other activists to bring about this change."

"Sign me up! You've got your first supporter and volunteer!" Autumn said enthusiastically. "In fact, let me be your partner in the movement. As you know, I have a lot to say about social injustice and disparity toward mental illness and mental disability."

"I'd love it if you joined me!" Ginger said warmly.

"You can put down our names as well, but wow, that's an ambitious undertaking, trying to bring about that kind of change," Daehan said, taking everything in.

She smiled as she pictured him as a young man with the walkie-talkie and the rifle heading up to be a lookout on their parents' roof.

"What can I say? I learned by watching those I love do the same."

Daehan nodded slowly, understanding the full meaning of her words.

"As soon as you're ready and the danger from COVID is over, I'll travel with you to give speeches and do outreach," Autumn said.

"Great, let's discuss this more tomorrow," Ginger said.

"Absolutely. I'm so excited," Autumn said. "Right now though, I've got to get the dishes cleared away and take care of the boys. They're getting a bit restless."

They all said goodnight to Autumn and the boys. A minute later, it was just Ginger, Daehan, and Mary on the call together.

"You know, trying to bring about change, no matter what route you take, isn't easy," Daehan said somberly.

"Brother, I'm well aware. I haven't forgotten what it cost you. I've also learned a lot through my struggles. It is like fighting to breathe when your lungs are already compromised."

Mary quietly took her husband's hand. "We're just worried for you," she said softly.

"I know, but don't be, please. I'm going to finally do what I was never able to do for all these years."

"What's that?" Daehan asked.

"I'm going to stand up!"

ABOUT THE AUTHOR

Jong Yi was born in the small, beautiful fishing and farming village of Chungnam, South Korea. Yi came to North America in 1985. While she attended Adult Basic Education and English as Second Language classes, she worked as a waitress in her sister's small mom-and-pop restaurant in Bethell, Alaska. Later, Yi began working in nursing homes as a Certified Nurse's Assistant while she studied the Arts. After Yi earned her associate degree in Arts, she pursued nursing and became a Registered Nurse. Yi has been a nurse since 2003 in the United States.

Made in the USA
Columbia, SC
30 May 2021